The Lost Few

by

Kimberlee R. Mendoza

The Lost Few

Cover Art by *Kim Mendoza*

The Wild Rose Press, Inc.
PO Box 708
Adams Basin, NY 14410-0708
Visit us at www.thewildrosepress.com

Publishing History
First Crimson Rose Edition, 2017
Print ISBN 978-1-5092-1744-1
Digital ISBN 978-1-5092-1745-8

Published in the United States of America

Dedication

To Theodore (Teddy) Shriver.
You were a beautiful baby taken too early in this life.
Not "forgotten" or "lost," but forever in our hearts.

"Get down,"

Myers yelled as he vaulted behind a metal cabinet. The office windows exploded into shards of glass. Several pelted his bare forearms and face. He blocked out the sting to find where his girlfriend landed.

Denise had dropped under a desk. Several bullets pelleted the leather chair behind it. "We're completely surrounded. Where's Laura?"

Myers pitched a stapler at the gunman. It smacked against his forehead. The burly man yelped and stumbled back. He growled and swung the submachine gun back toward Myer's position, spraying bullets against the cabinet.

Not good. Myers pressed back desperately against the concrete wall. His empty pistol clanked to the floor. He glanced back to Denise.

Her brown eyes darted around the room in frantic desperation. "She should be here by now. We've got to go!"

He pulled his line of site from her and surveyed the corporate office. Behind them was a three-story drop to the parking lot. Not many options. "Got a rope?"

"Network cable?" Denise yanked a blue wire and held it in the air.

The barrage of bullets ceased.

Myers peeked.

The gunman unclipped the magazine from his gun and went to reload a fresh one.

No hesitation. Myers toppled the heavy steel cabinet onto him.

The man buckled under it.

Now to get out of here.

Praise for Kimberlee R. Mendoza

"Mendoza writes with the mind of a chess champion. She's always at least three moves ahead of her reader."
~Paul McShane from Good News

Prologue

According to the BBC*, there are currently an estimated three hundred thousand child soldiers in the world, most in places like Sierra Leone, Liberia, Congo, Sudan, Sri Lanka, Afghanistan, and Burma.

For two decades in Uganda, ninety percent of the soldiers who fought in their various wars were children. Children are small and can infiltrate tight spaces undetected. Children seem innocent and are less likely to be a target. Children can be taught, blackmailed, and brainwashed. And in some cultures, children are unimportant and expendable.

In 1989, a former C.I.A. agent, Mel Greenstone, returned from Africa with an epiphany for a black ops unit like none the U.S. Government had ever seen. However, he wasn't able to convince several high-ranking officials to implement his plan—to recruit orphans, homeless teens, and young criminals to a secret organization and train them as special agents. He decided to take matters into his own hands. With a few financial backers, he created S.I.U.—the Secret Intelligence Unit.

In Greenstone's words, "Young people without a real future will be given one as the next generation of soldiers."

Years later, six of these soldiers fought back and imprisoned Greenstone, believing the head of the snake had been cut off. Desiring a normal life and to stop running, they were determined to prove their freedom. Until then, they would be the lost few.

****

*http://www.bbc.co.uk/worldservice/people/feature s/childrensrights/childrenofconflict/soldier.shtml

Chapter One

"Get down," Myers yelled as he vaulted behind a metal cabinet. The office windows exploded into shards of glass. Several pelted his bare forearms and face. He blocked out the sting to find where his girlfriend landed.

Denise had dropped under a desk. Several bullets pelleted the leather chair behind it. "We're completely surrounded. Where's Laura?"

Myers pitched a stapler at the gunman. It smacked against his forehead. The burly man yelped and stumbled back. He growled and swung the submachine gun back toward Myer's position, spraying bullets against the cabinet.

Not good. Myers pressed back desperately against the concrete wall. His empty pistol clanked to the floor. He glanced back to Denise.

Her brown eyes darted around room in frantic desperation. "She should be here by now. We've got to go!"

He pulled his line of site from her and surveyed the corporate office. Behind them was a three-story drop to the parking lot. Not many options. "Got a rope?"

"Network cable?" Denise yanked a blue wire and held it in the air.

The barrage of bullets ceased.

Myers peeked.

The gunman unclipped the magazine from his gun and went to reload a fresh one.

No hesitation. Myers toppled the heavy steel cabinet onto him.

The man buckled under it.

Now to get out of here. Myers eyed the same network cable running the length of the carpet by his left foot. He tugged hard, and the cord snapped free on his end. He tied it around the desk leg and jerked the cable. The knot held. *Perfect.* "Toss a computer out the window, and we're outta here."

With a nod, Denise complied and lobbed the monitor through the already broken window. The remaining glass rocketed in shards toward the bushes below.

More bullets flickered across the space from the bloodied gunman who had somehow freed himself.

Myers ran for her position and tackled her out the window, holding nothing more than her and the wire. Gravity pitched them back toward the building. *This is going to hurt.* He tensed as they smashed violently against the second-story window. Its stubborn frame sent pain through his arm, the glass remaining completely intact.

In unison, the couple let go and dropped to the clump of bushes below. Sticks shoved into his side and legs. Ignoring the damage, Myers dragged himself from the bushes with Denise and said, "Keep moving."

****

Laura swerved past lanes of cars in a mad haste. The lot was packed. An opening pulled her attention. With a single rotation of the steering wheel, she swerved her black SUV into a vacant parking space.

She flipped the visor mirror down, not a line of makeup out of place. A blur of two figures appeared in the corner of the review mirror. With instinct, she curved her hand around the gun under her seat. The figures came into focus. Myers and Denise. The two raced across the parking lot waving feverishly. *Act now, ask later.* Letting go of the gun, she cranked the gearshift into reverse. The tires screeched as it shot out from the parking space. With a hard right, the vehicle swung to a halt within feet of the pair.

They vaulted into the back and slammed the door.

Bullets showered the side of the car.

Laura flattened the gas pedal and accelerated across the crowded parking lot and out of the driveway. She vetted for every distance advantage before the assailants could enter in pursuit. Dust kicked into the air as the SUV broke from the paved road onto a dirt path. Hopefully, the dust cloud wouldn't aid the enemy in finding them. Laura weaved between idle tractors and freshly laid concrete foundations. New house frames of construction cultivated toward the center of the community. Its young nature meant less people, the perfect place to operate—both for the enemy and them.

The road behind remained vacant, so it appeared they were alone. *For now.* "What happened?" Laura demanded. "What'd you do?"

"Yeah, sure, we're fine," Myers retorted at her frustrated reflection in the review mirror. His gold-brown eyes glared at her.

"Sorry, occupational hazard." She inhaled deeply and looked at them in fast segments over her right shoulder. "Are you both okay?"

"A little banged up, but we'll live." Myers

dislodged a fragment of glass from his bicep and blood trickled down his arm.

"We did as you said." Denise plucked several twigs from her boyfriend's bundle of dread locks. "This morning, we started our new jobs in the credit department. Myers had barely put a thumb drive in, when an alarm sounded, the office cleared out, and this burly man with a gun came in."

Laura's fist struck the steering wheel. "So, we were right. Madison and Clark is indeed a shell company." News that Laura had wanted—no, needed—to be wrong. The notion that S.I.U. still had working cells made everything more complicated, not to mention deadly. They couldn't start a new life until they could rid the world of the unit's existence. Until that day, they would always be looking over their shoulders.

Myers leaned forward, checking his reflection as he tied a bandana around his head. "What does that mean now?"

"It means we go into hiding until we can come up with a plan." Laura turned down another back road and hit a hard bump. The car jolted.

Myers head hit the roof by her.

"Sorry."

Myers audibly sighed. "So, our plan to live normal lives is now in the wind."

"Hate to say it, but yeah, for now." Laura pushed a button on her visor, and a garage door slid open. She rolled in and cut the engine. The door dropped closed behind her.

Charlie entered the open doorway munching on a sandwich. His shoulder-length blond hair was matted and messy like he'd just woke up. "I like what you did with the car."

Laura came around to the passenger's side and surveyed the bullet holes. "Yeah, I thought you would. Where are Eri and Bryce? We need to have a team meeting."

"Tragically making lunch," Charlie said, stepping back so they could enter. "That's why I made my own."

"That is tragic." Denise grimaced. "Is the house on fire?"

Eri met them just inside the hall, arms crossed and with an annoyed scowl. "You want to eat? Because you don't have to, even though I make the best salt and pepper shrimp in Los Angeles."

"Good thing we're in Colorado." Denise winked. "Those blackened hockey pucks we ate last time…what was that again?"

"Tacos," Eri said.

"Yeah, if you say so."

"Look, I grew up in Chinatown. We didn't eat Mexican food."

Bryce leaned in the doorway, chewing. "Eri's right. It's pretty good this time."

His presence still made Laura's heart flutter. Muscular, dark hair, intense blue eyes—it was nice coming home to him. She set her case on the counter and crossed to her man. Aftershave wafted to her nose increasing the beat of her heart. She leaned for a slow kiss. "Hello."

He smiled. "Welcome back."

"Let's eat before it gets cold," Eri said with a thicker accent. They had all noticed that the more Eri got frustrated, the more her accent came out. It was always a sign to listen.

"Good idea." Laura wrapped her arm under Bryce's arm and strolled with him into the dining room. "I'm starved." Bowls of gourmet Chinese food lay on the table. Noodles with pork or chicken, she wasn't sure which. Beef with vegetables. Walnut shrimp. Appetizers. It could have come from any Chinese restaurant. "This looks good."

"It is." Eri shook her head and sat on the end, motioning for others to follow. "So I can't make a good taco, but this I can do."

Denise and Myers slid into the seats across from Laura and Bryce, leaving Charlie to sit at the other end across from Eri. After the morning they had, it didn't take long for everyone to fill their plate, ready to devour this food—good or bad. Lucky for them, it was delicious.

"So, what happened out there?" Bryce asked before biting into a pot sticker.

Laura set her chopsticks down and glanced at Myers.

"The company was rigged." His jaw clenched. "We no sooner accessed that file and they were on us. Laura didn't even get to park the car."

"That's great." Eri grimaced. "What do we do now?"

The question of the day. What now? It became common for this group to look to her for guidance. Occasionally, as a joke, they called her "Mama Black." Per usual, they expected her to know everything. Could she admit that just maybe this time she didn't know what to do? Spying, running, and killing—that is what she knew. Hiding and protecting others—not her style. But it was what she agreed to the minute she left S.I.U.

These young people needed her. Except for Bryce, they were all technically still teenagers. Most kids their age were worrying about prom and picking a college. These poor kids would never have those worries. They would always be looking over their shoulders, praying for another day alive. The real miracle would be living to have teenagers of their own someday. That is, if Laura could find a way to bring down anyone left to kill them.

"I don't quite understand." Eri took a sip of tea, then asked, "I thought S.I.U. died with Greenstone."

To be honest, Laura had wished and prayed for the same thing. "The leadership is destroyed, but it's like a snake." Laura bit into a shrimp and savored the sweet sauce, before continuing. "The body is still moving. If we aren't careful, it might grow another head."

Chapter Two

Myers flipped off the TV and stared at his beautiful girlfriend. The blue streaks were almost gone out of her black hair, which was piled up high in a spray of strands. Large hoop earrings hung from her ears and a small diamond decorated her nose. Her golden brown eyes danced with private thoughts that he often couldn't read. Even though they'd been together for almost six months, he still had trouble getting her to trust him. He couldn't blame her. The last time she trusted someone, she ended up in federal custody.

"I'm sorry, what did you say?" Myers asked.

"I think it's time." Denise wrapped her arms around a tan square pillow and tucked her knees under her on the matching couch.

"Time for what?"

She hit him in the chest lightly with the pillow.

He pretended to be hurt. "Sorry, I'm not following."

She drew his dark hand into hers and stroked it. Their skin colors clashed in beautiful contrasting hues. "To get out of here. To go."

"To go?" He glanced at the hallway, hoping Laura wasn't in earshot. "Go where, Denise?"

"Myers, we've been here for months. Three months in fact, for what? Nothing is happening. No one is coming. Aren't you ready to get back to our lives? To stop hiding." She kissed his cheek and half-grinned. "To be our own people. With people we love."

He scooted back sideways on the couch to face her. "We can't go home. Laura said—"

"I know what Laura said. I'm not talking about that. I'm talking about us—you and me—starting our own life somewhere else. Off the radar. You're really the only person I trust in this entire world." She leaned in and whispered, "You're it for me, babe."

His lips touched hers—soft and passionate. His heart swelled with love. "You're it for me too."

"Then let's just do it. Get out of here. Marry or something."

He sat back with a raised eyebrow. "Marry?"

Denise dropped his hand. "What? Didn't you mean it?"

Not a good tone, it was one he'd come to recognize as a warning. Denise was a lot of things—rational when angry was not always one of them. "No, it's just...I'm only eighteen. You're still a minor—"

"By six months. Look, we may seem like simple teenagers to some, but in experience, not even close. Not many teenagers endure what we've endured. Seen what we've seen. Make choices like we do. We lost our innocence a long time ago. We look, think, and act more mature than most thirty year olds. And technically, we're even older, because we have forged documents that say otherwise." She rolled her shoulders. "What's the problem?"

There were too many issues to concretely name one. He stood and paced. His mind crowded with rambling thoughts and questions. How did he explain the panic that this conversation just started? Leave

Laura and their friends? That encapsulated many issues. Whether their team admitted it or not, they could easily be deceiving themselves into thinking they were safe. Look at what happened just this morning. Today, they could have died. Who says those people aren't still looking for them? To marry into all this—it was insane. Not to belabor it, but they were young. Marriage was for life. At least, that was how he was raised. Six months was not long enough to know for sure.

"I don't get why you're stressing this." She swung away from him and pushed back into the couch, arms crossed and lips pursed.

He turned toward her, calculating each movement with caution. Did he tell her what his mind was really thinking and risk an argument? Or just go along with it for now? No, he was done with lies. The answer was simple. The few members who had survived made a pact to be honest. That inherently rolled over into his relationship with Denise.

"I don't want you to be mad. And I know you. You will be." He shuffled his hands together, like someone getting ready to catch a ball.

She licked her lips and looked at him with an expression that didn't match her words. "Okay, I promise to listen and hear what you're saying."

"I'm afraid to leave. I'm afraid to marry."

Their eyes locked, and the room fell silent.

Would she yell?

The clock in the den ticked rhythmically with each off beat, punctuating every anxiety-ridden moment. A train rumbled in the distance, pounding steel tracks in tandem with his heart.

Denise's expression was blank; her mouth was

quivering.

He fought the psychological bonds that trapped his voice. The clock, train, heartbeat—all of them flowed together as a chorus. A red dot flickered against Denise's forehead. The air shuttered with a pop. The window ruptured. Blood sprayed. Denise fell limp to the floor, as the chorus of noise melded into a single cry of grief.

Myers dropped to his knees, gripped with horror. Frozen. The room blurred. Sounds muffled.

The door flew open. Instinctively, he reached for Denise. He crumpled with her in his grasp. A dark stream of blood rushed from a hole above her left eye.

Someone stood behind him. Myers didn't turn to find out whom.

"Run!" came Charlie's voice with a murmur against the rhythm of the place.

The walls spun. All sensation left Myer's body. No tears. No fear. Only numbness held him. His body lay heavy on Denise's, saturated by warm liquid and a lifeless body.

More shouts echoed from Charlie—indiscernible words. His arms flailed, waving to the door. Myers stayed, knitted to his love. Denise's eyes, still open, were rolled back, unresponsive. He brought his lips to hers. Cold, gone. He clung in desperation to his disbelief.

Charlie wrestled Myer's arm to stand. "Man, we have to move!"

"Denise…" The word glided with his breath.

His friend lifted her limp body and began tugging her out the door. Myers followed. Small explosions of debris rippled throughout the room like confetti. Myers and Charlie brushed the walls to a hurried crouch and leapt into the hallway.

Laura and Eri also knelt there, facing opposite ends of the hallway, guns poised.

Myers reached out to help support Denise.

"Let's go!" Laura kicked back the door across from them and motioned toward it.

They poured into the room with her.

Myers progressed forward on rubbery legs; the room twisted in a blurred haze. His legs buckled underneath him, causing him to drop part of Denise.

"You have to leave her," Laura said.

Myers rebelled. "No way!"

"She'll slow you down. You'll die too."

Her words carried little weight. There was no chance he'd leave Denise while he still drew breath.

Laura shook her head and jerked the access closed. Footsteps clicked up the stairs below. With a convicted gaze, their leader thwacked her gun against the opposing window until it gave way, peering down as the shards fell.

"Balcony, no fire escape, short drop. Everyone out!" Without hesitation, she vaulted out the window and out of sight.

"Go ahead, man. I've got this," Charlie said, pulling Denise over his shoulder. His eyes sent slight reassurance.

Myers nodded and flared his legs out the window. He buckled as he hit hard against the earth. He shot up quickly and glanced up to Charlie, who lowered Denise over the edge. Myers held his arms out. Her body rammed against him, sending him back to the ground. Blood smeared against his chest and forearm. Unphased, he grunted to his feet. Instinct pulsed him forward.

Charlie landed next to Myers and aided in carrying Denise.

Eri jumped next and rolled into a crouched position by their side. "We have to keep moving."

A SUV, manned by Bryce, skirted to their position.

The group piled in. Myers clutched Denise's head in his lap. He brushed her matted hair from her face and scrubbed harshly to wipe the crimson stain away with the corner of his jacket. His tears mixed with her blood. Without rest, the SUV buzzed continuously forward. Voices of concern, forlorn comfort, and anger filled the cabin—but the sounds fell deafly on Myers's ears. He only saw Denise, the love of his life, motionless in his arms. Why hadn't he agreed to marry her?

Chapter Three

Laura closed her eyes and tried to still her breathing. Anger raged through her system. This death was on her. It was her idea to go into the corporation and steal intel. Why had she been so hasty? They should have done more recon. She exhaled slowly and opened her eyes. Maybe it was time to let the company go—to move on with their lives. Bryce and she could marry and live happily ever after in some island resort or desolate forest cabin. Why were they trying to fight this never-ending battle? The intel they collected on S.I.U. told them one thing—they only cut off the tail of the snake. Greenstone was only a pawn, not the player she had assumed owned all of the company. But who did? Did it matter?

"Pull in there." Eri pointed to a construction project next to what appeared to be an abandoned warehouse. Several bulldozers, two backhoes, a cement truck, and a dump truck all lay at the foot of a mound of dirt.

Bryce pulled around behind the old building, before parking and cutting the engine next to a bulldozer. Once the car was still, he faced Myers. His gaze dropped to Denise. "What happened?" His voice shaky, revealing his grief.

Tears burned Laura's throat and eyes as she tried to assess the situation. Their friend laid dead and their other friend was inconsolable, wracked with visible emotion. The small space fell dormant and thick. No one spoke for a while. The only sound came from the quiet whimper of Myers as he sobbed into the chest of his lost friend.

Eri wrapped her arm around his shoulder and rested her head against his arm. "I'm so sorry. We all loved her."

"What happened?" Bryce asked again through tears.

"She was fine. We were talking and a laser…" Myers voice cracked. He lightly caressed the back of her cheek with his knuckle.

"This sucks!" Charlie shoved the door open and dropped to the ground. Pacing around the car, his frustration could be heard through grunts and choice words.

"One thing is for certain, they are going to pay," Myers said through gritted teeth.

Laura felt relieved at that statement—basically because she needed him to be in fight mode, if they were going to get through this.

"We need to find a place to bury her. We can't take her to the authorities. As far as they are concerned, she is already dead." No one responded, so Laura continued, "Once she is buried, I think we need to split up."

"Is that wise?" Charlie poked his head inside. "Won't they pick us off one-by-one?"

She shook her head. "We are too big a target right now. We need to blend in more." Laura stared at Bryce. Worry clouded his eyes. She knew his thoughts without him voicing them. He was afraid she'd leave him. Though that did seem to be the sane thing to do, she would not allow herself to give into that instinct. "Bryce and I will stay together. The three of you can decide how you want to disperse."

Eri glanced from Myers to Charlie. Her thoughts masked with no emotion.

Myers obviously didn't care. His purpose and his teammate were gone.

"I'll stay with Myers," Charlie said. "Eri, if any of us could make it alone, you can. But you're welcome to come with us."

She shook her head, her black-bob swinging side-to-side. "Yes, I would be fine alone. My family has places where a woman can disappear. But I would rather stay with you for now, if that is okay."

He nodded.

Laura glanced once more at Denise, her face now ashen, devoid of life. How Laura's heart ached. She needed to be *doing*—doing anything other than grieving. She pulled a metal first-aid kit from under the seat and opened the latch. Inside were fake I.D.s and money. She handed each person his or hers. Though she didn't used to cry, emotion came easier now. Her eyes welled with tears as she looked at Denise. She stepped from the vehicle and wiped her face with her sleeve, before leaning back in. "I think our provisional backpacks are in the trunk."

"Yeah, I packed them a few weeks ago," Charlie said.

"Where should we bury her?" Myers whispered.

Laura searched the dirt lot. Her eyes fell on a bulldozer next to a mound a few yards away. "There. It looks fresh. We can dig it back up, put her inside, and then replace the dirt."

"No headstone?" Eri asked.

"We do not exist," she said. The glances that eyed her were less than approval. "We'll come back someday and make this about her. For now, it is the best we can do."

Myers slowly stepped from the vehicle and cradled her to the spot. Charlie and Bryce labored to recreate the hole. Once it seemed deep enough, Myers kissed her lips and placed her softly inside. "Yes, I will marry you, Denise. My fear was always about losing you, never about loving you. I will miss you terribly." He moved back and dropped to his knees.

"Thank you, Denise, for everything." Eri dropped a handful of dirt inside. "You were a beautiful woman, my friend. Rest in peace."

Charlie took a deep intake of air and exhaled loudly before saying, "Go with God, Denise. Know you were loved."

Bryce and Laura said their good-byes and then nodded to Charlie to cover her with the dirt inside the bucket of a bulldozer. Within seconds, all that remained was a pile of earth. Each hugged another's neck, the mood solemn, the reality sadder still.

"Remember our code, should we need help?" Laura said.

Charlie nodded. "The fake dating service is still in effect. We'll be monitoring it."

Laura nodded. "If anyone is in trouble, being followed, hurt, whatever, use it."

Bryce took her hand in his and led her to the car.

Charlie hotwired an old van in the lot and got into the driver's seat. Myers dropped next to Charlie and waved to them. Eri slid into the back and slammed the door closed.

Climbing into the car, Laura didn't know when things would be okay again. She had wished for so much more. This may have ended any hope of happiness. How would Myers go on? Would they always be running? If only she could go back and tell them to forget the past, and just start the future. But the "if only" game was not helping her now. She needed to roll it off and find safety.

"Do you know where you want to go?" Bryce asked, as the engine roared to life.

"I can think of only one place."

He tilted his head, obviously waiting for an answer.

"And you're not going to like it."

Chapter Four

Eri stared at the contents of the back of the van—a dirty mattress, old cans of food, and empty containers. This must have been a homeless person's hideout. She slid on her knees to the front to see the road. Myers appeared broken. His normally dark brown face ashen, cheeks caressed with fresh tears. She rubbed his arm.

He touched her hand and turned to face the window.

What did they do now? She glanced at Charlie in the review mirror.

His eyes met hers. "You have any ideas about where we should go?" he asked. "You said things about people disappearing."

There were places. Places for people like her. But would they accept her new friends who were clearly not part of that community? And did they exist to her any longer? After all, she was—for all intents and purposes—dead. Those connections may be severed. Worse, they could be compromised. "We can try. Do you know Chinatown in LA?"

"That's a two day drive from here."

Eri patted his shoulder. "Yes, but that is the best I know."

"Would it be better to avoid crowded places?" Myers asked, not turning to them.

"No, I don't think so. We need to disappear in the

crowd," Eri said.

Charlie used a free hand to adjust his beanie. "Okay, you're the boss. We all know you're the smartest one here."

Eri laughed. Myers and Charlie were both computer hackers and ingenious criminals; she was simply a martial artist, hardly the one with the brains. "Ha! You two are the brains. I'm the brawn."

Charlie laughed.

Normally, Myers would take offense, but he didn't respond in any way. How could he? Her heart felt extremely heavy for him. She laid her head on his shoulder and closed her eyes. The sound of the road could have lulled her to sleep if her mind wasn't so plagued with Denise's murder. She had lost lots of people, but this one was different. It left a hole in her soul. No one knew she was there when it happened. But she saw it. Just seconds before, she had come into grab a candle. She overheard the word "marry" and hid behind the wall to eaves drop. The vision of the bullet hitting her friend's head just played over and over in her memory.

"Are you okay?" Charlie said.

She glanced at his reflection.

"Sure, why?"

"You're crying."

Eri touched her cheek. Tears. She hadn't even noticed. Had she become so hard she couldn't even understand her own emotions when they were happening. She slid a sleeve over her face and shifted in the van. Her knee touched a black banana peel. She winced and tossed it farther back. "Not the classiest of vehicles."

"It was available." Charlie signaled to switch lanes. "We'll upgrade later."

"I've been thinking… I'm not sure that people in Chinatown can help us."

His gaze shot to her and then back to the road. "Why not?"

"I'm dead, remember?"

Charlie turned to stare at her.

"Watch the road, Charlie," she said.

"Well, I'm open to suggestions. Where do we go?"

"It depends," Myers said, not facing them.

"On what?" Eri asked.

"On whether or not we want to live normal lives or kill the jerks who did this to Denise." He kicked the floorboard of the van and stared out the side window.

"We've been fighting. Look what that is doing. Maybe it is time we hide." Eri sat back and pulled her knees to her chest.

Myers flipped around in his seat and faced her. "You don't believe that. Please tell me you don't believe that."

"We need to make a choice," Charlie said.

Eri sighed. "Fine, you're right. We all know that choice A does not exist. There is nothing normal left for us. We also know choice B would get us killed."

"But is there a C?" Charlie turned off the road into a rest stop, parked, and shut off the engine. "Couldn't we go find some place to lay low? Some place way off the radar?"

"Seriously, C? Holing up like a bunch of scared rabbits?" Myers eyes narrowed.

"It doesn't mean we are cowards. It just gives us time—" Charlie started.

"I vote for killing." Myers slammed opened the door and jumped out of the van.

Eri slid the back open and walked to his side.

Charlie joined them.

"The reality is we have to do all three. We need Charlie's Plan C first so we can plan. And, we have to do B, if we ever want A. Make sense?"

"Plan, kill, live." Charlie smiled. "I like that." He pulled his beanie from his head and ruffled his blond hair sending it standing in multiple directions. "So where do we go? Chinatown?"

"Wait." Myers squatted to the ground. He picked up a tiny rock and tossed it against a metal trashcan a few feet away. "I think I know a place."

****

They drove all day. Charlie did most of the driving, but at one point, Myers took over so he could get them to their destination. The sun had just begun to sink behind the horizon when the van stopped in a group of trees along the road.

Eri wiped her eyes and tried to get her bearings. "Where are we?" She slid out of the passenger seat and looked to a paved driveway up the road.

Charlie walked ahead to a brown and beige sign at the entrance. "A historical monument."

Eri joined him. The sign read: Petrova Estate, Built 1879, National Historical Park & Museum. She glanced up at the three-story Tudor mansion that stretched before them. Exterior lights were on, but the inside appeared dark. The windows were stained glass and the walkways cobblestone. Lush bushes ran the property, indicating someone kept it up. The place was expensive and old—but more importantly, not a real residence.

"Myers, what is in your head?"

"My best friend in high school used to talk about this place all the time. It's not open to the public this time of year." He nodded to a sign with hours that read, *Closed for the Winter.* "The guys used to hang out here on weekends. Never encountered anyone."

A bad feeling swept through her body. The last thing they needed was to get arrested for trespassing on government property. "Security? Cameras?"

"I don't think so." Myers reached for his backpack in the back of the van. "My friend said no one came up here. He was always trying to talk me into coming to one of his parties."

Still not convinced, Eri ran back and grabbed her own backpack. "Well, I can't say I am thrilled."

"Sorry, it was the only place I could think of that no one else would think of, you know what I mean?"

Together, they walked up the driveway.

Myers walked to the front door and tried the handle. "It will have beds. If nothing else, we can just sleep for the night."

"Locked?"

He nodded.

Eri glanced at Charlie.

A sweet smile crept across his face. He lived for the break in. Though Myers was the resident thief, he had been training Charlie. The man was an instant natural and loved it. Charlie reached in his backpack, withdrew a small, black tool kit, and went to work on the lock.

"How do we know we won't set off some silent alarm?" Eri asked.

Charlie stopped and reached into his backpack for

a tablet. "Give me a second."

Myers nodded. "I should have thought of that."

"But you didn't." Charlie laughed. "There. We're good."

Eri glanced over his shoulder. "What did you do?"

"Hacked into the alarm and disarmed it." He flipped the case closed on his tablet and stuffed it back in his pack, before going to work on the door again.

Complete awe. "How do you guys do this stuff?"

Myers didn't smile. "We just do."

The lock turned, and the door cracked open. Charlie stepped back and bowed as if he worked as a butler. "After you."

They stumbled in. The room was dark and smelled of old books and mildewed tapestries. Eri pulled out a flashlight and scanned the space. A Victorian looking lamp stood to her left. She turned a key on its side, and it flickered on. In front of them was a long, carved, cherry wood hall. On the left was a sunken living room decorated in cream Victorian-style décor. On the right was a large library filled wall-to-wall with books. At the end of the large hall was a staircase. Behind it was what appeared to be a formal dining room.

"I don't think we should keep the light on?" Charlie said.

"There isn't anyone for miles," Myers replied.

"Still?" Charlie asked.

Eri turned her flashlight back on, snapped off the lamp, and moved toward the daunting staircase. It reminded her of *Gone With the Wind*. She half expected Scarlet O'Hara to come flying down the staircase any moment yelling about Tara.

Each step creaked in resistance. The old wood roof

groaned as it settled, making frightening sounds.

"This place is something else," Charlie whispered. "Do you believe in ghosts?"

"Don't be ridiculous." Myers smacked the back of him.

"Well, I had to ask."

They reached the top of the staircase and pointed the flashlight down a long corridor. There were more than a dozen doors, all closed.

"Shall we?" Myers walked to the first door and tried the handle. It opened to a large bedroom, revealing a four-poster bed, lush carpets, a fireplace, and a desk. The air was thick and cool.

Eri passed him and opened the next door. A nursery. She crossed the hall and opened another door. It was similar to the one Myers had opened first. "I'll sleep in here."

Charlie passed her and opened the next door. "I'm in here."

Myers grunted, walked in his door, and shut it.

"I guess he's in there." Charlie laughed, walked in, and shut his own door.

Eri entered and fumbled for a light. The first lamp didn't turn on. She scanned the room with her flashlight. There weren't any other lamps, but there appeared to be a light overhead. That may be too much. She sat the flashlight on the floor and pointed it toward the ceiling. It illuminated the room.

The four-poster bed had a cream canopy and was decorated with satin and lace pillows. Most women would probably find this pretty. It made her want to vomit. No one would ever accuse her of being a girly-girl. She liked black and red décor, with sharp edges, nothing fancy. This was revolting. She climbed on top of the lacey bedspread, and dust puffed into the air, causing her to cough. She waved at the particles. "Great." She laid her head down on the pillows, casting more dust, and coughed again. "Lord, help me."

Slowly, she closed her eyes.

"Wake up!" came Charlie's voice from somewhere distant. "Eri, now!"

Eri's eyes shot open.

Charlie and Myers stood over her. Sunlight streamed in the room. Her flashlight was still on a few feet away. "What's wrong?"

"I made a mistake," Myers said, helping her to her feet. "There are people here."

"What kind of people?" Eri rubbed her face, trying to get her bearings.

"Museum kind."

Oh! Eri's brain turned on. She nodded, grabbed her light, and stuffed it in the backpack by the door. "Where are they now?"

"Walking room to room. We heard them come in." Charlie glanced down the hall.

"Are they looking for us?" Eri whispered, slowly closing the door, before tiptoeing behind them.

"I don't think so, but I'm not sure," Myers said, looking back and forth.

"Plans to get out of here?" Eri asked.

"I think we're winging it," Charlie replied.

With each creaking step, they all visibly winced. It was impossible to creep in this old house. "They have to know we're here," Eri whispered.

"Stay close to the wall," Myers said. "It may help."

At once, they all backed up to the wall and inched

forward. At the end of the hall, they looked over the side of the staircase. Voices could be heard coming from the dining area.

"Now what?" Charlie said.

A woman entered, but didn't shut the door.

There was no other way out. Eri took a deep breath and then whispered, "Run."

No one hesitated. They all sprinted for the open door. Behind them, they heard "Stop!" and confusion. They didn't stop. The van was their only focus. All three jumped in. Security and museum staff ran to the entrance, waving, calling, screaming.

"Get us out of here, Charlie," Eri yelled.

He hit the wires together under the dashboard, and the van sputtered to life. The security guard reached the driver's side. "Sorry, dude, no time to chat." Charlie peeled backward and spun the wheel hard.

Myers in the back of the van flew against the side. "Ouch! Watch it man."

"Sorry." Charlie hit the gas, and they flew onto the road, sending a spray of pebbles behind them.

Eri looked in the mirror. The security guard was on a radio, likely reporting them. "We need a new vehicle."

Chapter Five

Laura stepped off the plane. The sticky heat slammed against her skin, reminding her how much she hated this place. A quick glance at Bryce's scowl said he felt the same. They grabbed their backpacks from the tarmac and ran to a waiting taxi. "Camino negro, near Nalga De Maca," Laura said to the driver.

The driver nodded and pulled out of the dirt lot sending dust in their wake. Bryce stared out the window, obviously still not talking to her. He agreed to come, but not without words, and not without disdain. It was dangerous. Returning to Puerto Rico where the S.I.U. had trained her was insane. That was not a debatable topic. She agreed. It was stupid. But it was also the last place they would think to look for her. There had to be some merit to this decision.

"I'm sure the compound is empty," Laura tried again in the silence.

His gaze met hers, not convinced.

"Please don't be mad. You came. I appreciate that. But I don't want you angry either."

He shut his eyes and sighed. "I'm here because I know you would come with or without me." His eyelids slowly lifted, and a slight smile formed on his lips. "I would not let you come alone."

"So, you're not mad?"

With a soft touch, he drew her head to his shoulder.

"I was never mad. Just concerned."

The taxi pulled down a dark, unpaved road. Laura's heart accelerated. The landscape was now familiar with bad memories. Had it only been a year since she had left here? The car made another turn, and her senses went on high alert. The compound was not far. She could sense it. Every logical thought yelled run away. Though the compound wasn't their destination, just knowing it was there made her ill.

"Aquí," the driver said, as he slowed in front of her friend Julio's bamboo home.

Bryce leaned over the seat and paid the man a handful of pesos. They got out, grabbed their gear, and walked to the front door. Something was definitely wrong. The door was slightly ajar, and a dining room chair lay upside down on the porch. The two of them glanced at each other. Just coming from the airport, neither had a weapon. Guarded, Laura slid the door open with her toe of her boot. On the floor, between the living room and kitchen, Juan's corpulent frame lay in a pool of tacky blood. Laura ran to his side and checked his neck. It was cold and hard. He had been here for a while. A maggot ran across her finger. She shook it off and wiped her hand on a nearby kitchen towel.

A gunshot rang from the adjoining room.

Bryce fell back.

Laura screamed. "Bryce!"

"I'm okay." He touched his left shoulder and looked at his hand. A dot of blood appeared. "It just nicked me."

Both scanned the room. They needed weapons—now!

Laura low crawled to a drawer, slid a paring knife

to Bryce's side, and then reached for a utility knife. Not elegant, but it would have to do. She indicated with a nod of her head that he'd take left and she would take right. Another bullet pelted the wall behind them. They ducked, but kept inching forward. Laura mouthed with fingers held high, "Three, two, one."

Both jumped through the door and tackled an olive-skinned woman to the ground. The gun rattled to the floor next to Bryce. The woman fought, but they managed to wrangle her onto her stomach, pushing her head into the dingy beige carpet.

"Alto," she screamed.

"She wants us to stop," Bryce said.

Laura rolled her eyes. "Yeah, I'm sure she does."

"You're American?" The woman's voice was muffled by the dirty shag carpet.

"Yes."

"I'm sorry I shot at you then."

Laura rolled her over, but straddled her, keeping both arms above the girl's head. "What do you mean?"

"I am Julio's daughter, Helena. The men from the village…they came and killed my father. He did nothing wrong. My father said to wait for an American woman."

Laura locked on Bryce's gaze. She had no idea what that meant. He shrugged. She looked back to Helena. "You're assuming he meant me? Why?"

"He said Laura Black would save me."

Laura cringed at hearing her name. "How do you know I am Laura Black?"

"I've seen a picture." The woman rolled her eyes up, indicating something over her head.

A photo sat on a small dresser behind her. In it,

Laura smiled with Julio. She didn't remember that picture being taken. Nor did she understand what was happening. It had taken a lifetime to build a "trap meter," but Laura had one. "How could your father assume I was coming? I didn't know he was in trouble." Laura glanced at Bryce, making sure he caught her meaning.

"Suspicious," Bryce mouthed.

She nodded.

"He said you would just know," Helena said.

Bryce retrieved the gun a few feet away and pointed it in her direction.

Trap or no trap, Laura needed to know what was happening. She'd play along for now, but there was no way she could fully trust this. Laura backed up slowly and sat across from the woman on a twin size mattress. "I'm not sure if what you're saying is true. We were coming here to seek refuge from some bad guys. I am sad to see your father didn't make it. He was good to me."

Tears glided from Helena's coffee-brown eyes to her dirt-covered, tan face. Her long, black hair was in knots, and her movements indicated she was weak and likely dehydrated. "Are you hungry?"

She nodded. "I've been hiding here for three days, afraid to go in the kitchen. I've been living off my sister's secret stash."

A quick glance around the room indicated she was telling the truth. A canister with yellow liquid sat against the wall, and another jug of water that appeared almost empty lay on the other side. Several junk food wrappers littered the floor.

Laura stood and held out her hand. "I doubt they'll

be back. Come on."

The woman timidly took her hand and stood.

"What's your name again?" Bryce asked.

They walked into the kitchen and Laura began rummaging in the cupboards.

"Helena."

"Nice to meet you, Helena. I'm Bryce. And this is, as you already seem to know, Laura."

She nodded with a gentle smile.

Laura produced some tortillas and cheese from the fridge. She handed both to the girl, who was not shy in scarfing them down. She then poured her a glass of water, which Helena chugged. Satisfied that she had done the humane action, Laura now needed to get answers. "Now we need to figure out what to do. We came here to hide in Julio's bunker, but this may not be the best plan."

Bryce winked with a sarcastic smile.

"Okay, don't get all *I told you so* on me. I had no idea there would be some local issues going on." Laura glanced at the blood on Bryce's shirt. "Let's see it."

He slid his sleeve up. "See, only a scratch. I told you, nothing to worry about."

"Well, go clean it up." Laura glanced at their host. "Do you have rubbing alcohol?"

"Si, in the bathroom."

Bryce walked to the small room to their left, returning with a clear white bottle.

Knowing he was okay, Laura stared at Helena. "Do you know the S.I.U. compound? Are there people there?"

"I've never been, but I know about it. Father said to never go near it."

34

Laura glanced at Bryce with a knowing smile. "That was good advice."

"I think we need to check it out. If it is empty, it would be a great place to hole up." Bryce ripped a piece of tortilla off and plopped it in his mouth.

"And if it isn't?"

Bryce's gaze locked with hers. "Then you'll need another plan."

****

Laura crept forward to the edge of the gate and pointed for Helena to stay back. Bryce followed holding Helena's gun at his chest. The air lay quiet except for the chant of tree frogs and monkeys. The gate did not appear locked. Laura pushed, and it easily slid open.

Bryce motioned for her to go through.

She nodded and darted inside, quickly squatting behind the last barrier she had seen in this place—the tower. It now stood empty. Cobwebs and overgrowth covered the base. The lot stood barren and silent. Once both of them were in, she darted for the nearest building—the main bunker that used to house the offices, including Greenstone's. Ivy had grown up from the foundation enfolding the windows. She turned the handle. Locked. A few feet away was a broken window. She darted to it and peered inside. Shards of glass rested on the ground both inside and out. A desk sat underneath. "Raise me up," she whispered to Bryce.

He cupped his hands, and she stepped into them, boosting herself onto the desk inside.

"Ouch!" Bryce winced.

"What happened?"

He held his hand in the air and pulled out a tiny

piece of glass. "Glass from your boot."

"Sorry."

He grabbed Helena around the waist and lifted her up to Laura. Then both women pulled him in as he leveraged his boot against the wall.

The furniture inside appeared tossed, forgotten. It didn't seem anyone had been here for a while which allowed Laura to relax a bit. "Let's head for the main room. There are bathrooms and a kitchen."

Slowly, they made their way down the dark corridor, winding from hallway to hallway, checking each room as they went, and stating, "Clear." It seemed most of the place had been cleared out. A few tables and chairs were still around, most of them on their sides or up against windows for cover. Bullet holes adorned the walls. Empty smoke canisters and the occasional gas mask littered the floor. At the end, they found a metal door that housed the kitchen. Bryce pushed the door open and scanned the room. "Clear," he whispered.

Laura pulled a lantern she had taken from Julio's place from her pack and set it on the table. "Anyone have a match?"

Bryce opened a few cabinets and returned with a long lighter.

"That will work." Laura lit the lantern and turned the knob to brighten the room. Interestingly enough, the room did not seem like the rest of the building. The cupboards were filled with supplies and everything neatly placed in the drawers.

Helena slid onto one of the metal counters and opened a cupboard revealing spices. "What exactly did they do here?"

"Cook," Bryce said.

Helena laughed. "I meant at this facility, not the kitchen."

Bryce faced her. "I thought you said your dad told you about this place."

"He told me it was dangerous, that's it."

"It stole souls." Laura slid a couple of cans across the counter. "See if you can find an opener." She crossed to a row of drawers and began pulling them out. A chill swept through her, and a memory of this place dropped on her like a lead weight. How many nights had she come here with her old partner, Harding, to steal food? The memory of him laughing a few feet away, as he chugged mango juice, still resonated as if it was yesterday. There were some happy memories, but most were bad. Unable to control the emotions of this place, she folded to the ground.

Bryce ran to her side. "Are you okay?"

Am I? Feelings she hadn't suffered in so long consumed her like dead weight to her body. What was wrong with her? She didn't do this—lose control. Squeezing her eyes shut, she worked to still her breathing. "I am just having a panic attack. It is this place."

He held out his hand, and she took it to stand. "I know. Maybe we should go."

She shook her head. "I'll get over it. Just give me a second. Did you find an opener?"

Helena held one up.

Laura smiled, determined to push the feelings out. "Great. Let's eat."

****

Laura stared at the soldier's foot as he smashed

her cell phone with the heel of his boot.

"Who did you call?" the man yelled.

She spat in his face. Spittle ran down his cheek. He wiped it with his arm before smacking her cheek with the back of his hand. "Do you think you can play games?"

In the background, she saw Helena smiling. Why was she smiling?

Bryce was tied up, lying on the floor, covered in blood.

What had happened? How did they get here?

"All prisoners get one phone call, do they not?" Laura said.

"You keep making jokes, but I am not in a mood to play with you, girly. You will tell me who you called, or I will kill your boyfriend." The soldier laughed as he straddled Bryce, pulling his head back by the hair and revealing an exposed Adam's apple. Methodically, the soldier placed the knife at his throat. "Last chance."

Who did she call? She didn't know. She didn't remember calling anyone. "Your mama, perhaps."

The soldier sliced into his neck. Blood streamed out.

"No!" Laura screamed. What had she done?

Laura jumped up with a startled breath. Bryce lay on the bunk under her, Helena on a cot to her left. It had been a while since she had dreamed. When she remembered them that vividly, something bad usually happened. She slid down the side of the bunk, walked to the bathroom, and tossed some cold water on her face. Her eyes peered back red and tired; her face was far from rosy and healthy. A few white hairs stuck out with great contrast to her black short hair. Months of running had taken their toll. It was time to hide. To stop fighting. They all needed to regroup. So what if they could never do normal. They could at least relax somewhere, right? Why had she come here? Deep down, it had called to her. It trapped her. She kept coming back here. That had to stop. She had to go and never return. It was not healthy.

An office sat just to her left. She turned on the power strip and rebooted the computer. She logged into the dating service they had set up to correspond. There were a few ways they could communicate, but the easiest was to just send a message. Code words would be present, if she could remember all of them in her tired state. "Girl seeking guy who likes jungle adventure. Does not want to play games. Prefers to meet up at the start of something bad. Currently lives in the heat, but would like somewhere cold. Looking for Prince Charming. Don't delay. Ride in on your stallion." Send.

Now they wait.

Chapter Six

Eri tossed in the back of the sedan they boosted outside Redwood City. All night they had been driving. Twice, they had crossed state lines. No destination, just driving. The sky slowly turned a violet hue. The sun would rise soon. They needed to find cover.

"Let's stop here." Charlie pointed to a small hotel sign just off the highway.

"Sounds good."

He drove into the lot, then pulled out his laptop, and rigged them a free stay. Once again, Eri was amazed by his skills.

The room was not much to look at. The carpet was rust-colored shag carpet, and the walls were a mustard yellow trimmed by seventies-era wood paneling. A gaudy, flowered bedspread lay on the two queen beds. There was an old box TV, a small particle-wood table, and a worn bathroom that screamed bacteria. Gross or not, she needed a shower. She pulled fresh clothes from her bag and crossed to the bathroom. The warm water heightened every sense in her body. Never had something felt so relaxing. She tried not to stay in for too long, but it wasn't easy to leave. Within minutes of pruning, she turned off the faucet and dried. Inhaling the steam, she pulled on a clean shirt and her old jeans, before exiting the steam-filled room.

"You smell better." Charlie winked.

"You don't." Eri tossed a towel at him and thumbed for him to follow her example.

He waved and shut the door behind him.

Myers lay on the bed with Charlie's laptop.

Eri wound a towel on her head to dry the excess water and then joined him on the corner of the bed. "Is it okay to browse the Internet?"

"Charlie's computer is set with some safety nets." His mouth went wide, and he looked at her. "We have a message. Tell Charlie to hurry."

Eri walked to the door. She could hear the water running. "Charlie?"

The water stopped. "Yeah?"

"Hurry, we have a message."

"One sec."

Eri walked back to the bed and leaned over Myer's shoulder. His shirt was covered in blood and dirt. "You need a shower before we leave, too."

He glanced down. The pain of seeing the blood was probably a lot, but he said nothing. "Yeah, okay."

The bathroom door opened, and Charlie entered in only a towel. His chest was more chiseled than she remembered from before. She glanced away, but then peeked back and smiled.

"Dude, put some clothes on. There's a girl in here," Myers said.

Charlie grabbed the edge of his towel and pulled.

Eri screamed.

He wore shorts under the towel. Charlie and Myers laughed.

"Nice." Eri grimaced and tossed a pillow at his head.

"Sorry, I couldn't resist." He pulled a clean black

shirt from his bag and joined them on the bed.

Eri punched his arm.

"What's that for?"

"Sorry, I couldn't resist." She winked and turned back to the laptop.

She sensed his gaze on her, before moving to what they were all ready to see.

"Girl seeking guy who likes jungle adventure. Does not want to play games. Prefers to meet up at the start of something bad. Currently lives in the heat, but would like somewhere cold. Looking for Prince Charming. Don't delay. Ride in on your stallion."

"What does it mean?" Eri said.

Myers clicked his tongue on the roof of his mouth. "They're in Puerto Rico, but need us to come right away."

Eri shook her head. "How do you get that?"

"The jungle and start something bad is the old compound."

"And Prince Charming always comes and rescues them," Eri said. "Got it."

Charlie ran a hand through his wet hair. "Why do you suppose they are there?"

"No one would suspect we would go back." Myers put his hands to the keys. "How should I respond?"

That seemed too obvious. "Are they in danger?" Eri asked.

"I don't think so. Sounds like they are done running."

Eri looked at her friend. His brown eyes looked sad, but determined. "No one wants to fight right now. We all just need a break."

Myers slid out from under the laptop and set it on

the bed. "I'm going to take a shower."

"Myers?"

His gaze met Eri's. "Don't worry. I won't go rogue." The door closed.

Charlie wrapped his arm around her shoulder, and it felt surprisingly strong and comforting. With all that had happened, they hadn't had a chance to truly mourn their friend. Days, months, over a year of grief fell into the pot of emotions, and she began to cry heavily onto his shoulder. He stroked her hair softly, then his finger trailed down her cheek, and wiped her tears. Their eyes locked. Her heart raced. Sudden attraction came over her, and their lips met. Soft, inviting. He was kissing her. Charlie lips intertwined with hers. Salty, sweet, delicious. Every sense in her body relaxed. Was this really happening?

The water shut off in the other room.

Eri jumped back and stared at Charlie. Did that just happen? She started to speak, when the door opened. Both of them faced Myers. Guilty. Why did she feel like a kid caught stealing? She pushed up from the bed and awkwardly smiled. "So…when do we leave?"

****

Charlie worked hard to not smile. He had liked Eri from the minute he met her, but it wasn't something he would share. The truth was he was hardly a ladies' man. He often went stag or just hung out with friends. Girls had never noticed him. Or maybe it was all those hours gaming. Not many girls understood him. Eri was completely out of his league in the real world, but maybe here would be different. He hoped that was true.

"How are we going to get to Puerto Rico?" Eri asked, as they neared the airport. Myers opened his mouth, when Eri said, "Let me guess, Charlie booked us tickets?"

He glanced at her in the passenger seat and winked.

A slight blush washed over her cheeks, and she glanced out the side window. He wanted to kiss her again. But there was Myers to worry about. The guy just lost his girlfriend in the most awful way. The last thing Myers would want to see is two people making out. They would have to play this by ear—assuming Eri was even game.

They emptied their backpacks of weapons in a nearby trashcan just outside the Medford Airport. Within a few hours, they boarded and settled in for the eleven-hour flight. Charlie sat by the window, Eri in the middle, and Myers on the aisle, claiming longer legs. After take-off, Myers drifted to sleep. Eri's arm rested on the joined arm. Charlie's arm lightly touched hers. A tingling sensation swept up his spine. He sensed she felt the same, as her gaze met his.

He whispered, "Are we okay?"

Hidden beneath a sweatshirt, her fingers touched his. They toyed with each other's hands for a moment, before resting together. "We need to be careful." She glanced at Myers.

Charlie agreed.

She leaned her head on his shoulder and closed her eyes. Closing his eyes, he rested his head on top of hers. For the first time since he heard of S.I.U., he actually felt hope and happiness. There was no way he could hold onto this feeling, too much bad had happened. He knew that. But for the moment, he would enjoy it.

Chapter Seven

Laura nudged Bryce awake with a shake to his shoulder. "Someone's here."

Grabbing the gun by his side, he quickly joined her at the door of the barracks room. "Where?"

She nodded to the far left hall from where they entered. "I heard glass. Whoever it is, their coming in the way we did."

Bryce passed her and flipped around the wall and to the ground in a kneeling position.

Laura grabbed the Glock 42 pistol she had found earlier taped to the bottom of the director's desk. The hall appeared still. Her ears rang as they strained to hear. Three sets of feet, now detected, were moving their way. "Don't shoot unless we know who it is."

He nodded.

A birdcall came from Bryce. One they had practiced many times as a joke back in the apartment.

The call was returned.

"Your date has arrived," came Charlie's familiar voice around the corner.

Laura relaxed. Charlie, Eri, and Myers stood just feet away, smiling. She ran to hug each of them. They felt warm, like home. How had she got so completely attached to these people? How had she let them go?

"That's quite the welcome," Charlie said. "It hasn't even been a week."

Laura wiped her tears and grinned. "I shouldn't have told us to split up. We're family now. We stick together."

The three of their eyes went wide, smiles dissipated, as they took a step back.

Laura spun around, gun drawn.

Helena stood there, hands up.

Laura lowered her gun. "Oh, everyone this is Helena. A friend of mine's daughter."

"And I am so sorry," Helena said. "They gave me no other choice." She placed a gas mask on.

The air instantly grew thin. Laura's lungs seared. Confused. Angry. Scared. Her gaze shot to Bryce as she gasped for breath. He coughed violently, crumbling to the floor. His eyes rolled back into his head. The team all did the same. *Is this how it ends?* Why did she ask them here? Within seconds, everything went black.

****

The smell of ammonia made Laura wince. She labored to open her eyes. Blurry, she made out someone standing next to her holding something in his hand. She couldn't see his face clearly through a burlap bag over her head. Her wrists burned from what she detected as plastic ties. The faint smell of a burning cigarette also permeated the bag.

"Good, you're awake." The person pulled the bag hard, catching her hair and scratching her cheeks in the process. She lifted her gaze, squinting at the light, and her mouth fell open. *Greenstone? He's alive. He's here. Worse! He has me.*

"Agent Black, one of my best students." He wiped the sweat from his bald head, sat in a chair across from her, and took a strong drag from a brown cigarette. His peppered gray goatee and hair were shaved off, making his cheeks seem rounder than before.

"Shouldn't you be in prison?"

He chuckled. "Awe, my dear. Men in high places never fear those underneath their shoe." With one last puff, he flicked a cigarette to the floor and put it out with the toe of his boot.

"You bought your way out?" she said dryly. It figured. How could she be so delusional, to possibly think it would be that easy? Sure they showed him on national television, but a guy like Greenstone had the resources and power to disappear. Or start over. Her core grew numb. Had he started over? Or was he still up to his old tricks? *Training kids to be murderers.* Heat rose up her back. The desire to kill had never been so present.

His gaze bore into her. The man knew her almost as well as she knew herself. No doubt he sensed her hatred. How she loathed looking at him? It was like looking at an abusive father once you acknowledge the abuse. This man had stolen her childhood. Not in the conventional way some people endure, but stolen just the same. Revulsion radiated through her skull. Desperately, she wanted a gun.

"You look upset, Black."

How perceptive.

"If anyone should be angry, it should be me." He stood and crossed to a table filled with metal objects likely meant to bring her pain. He clicked his tongue. "Tisk, tisk, Black. I treated you like a princess, and you tried to have me destroyed."

"You took everything from me." Tears threatened to fall. This was not how she wanted him to see her—

broken. She blinked them back and steeled herself for the battle ahead.

He turned back to her, eyes cold. "What did you have? Nothing. I rescued you. Gave you a life. A career. Even a leadership position."

"It wasn't right," she spat, angry tears now falling.

"For whom? You? We should have terminated you when we had the chance." He sighed. "Something I can, and will, remedy now. But not easily. The punishment must fit the crime." A long vial in his hand squirted some liquid. He held it up like a trophy and brought it to her neck. She tried to wiggle away, but he grabbed her hair and yanked hard. She winced in pain. The needle jammed into the side of her throat. It burned. Her mind began to whirl. The room swayed. Nausea waved through her stomach. She blinked rapidly to clear her head, to no avail.

"I'll be back soon, and we'll begin," he said through the fog.

Whatever he had given her was fast and inhibiting any chance to concentrate. She needed clarity to discern her situation. Working to vomit, she focused on the nausea. It worked. She was able to let it all go on the floor. It didn't seem to clear her mind. Dumb. It wasn't a drink; it was a shot. In her blood stream. It was apparent her brain wasn't working well.

Greenstone entered and grunted at bile on the floor. "It's in your bloodstream, Black, not your mouth. Vomiting won't work." Of course, he knew her thought process. He practically raised her. He yelled out the door. "Get in here and clean this up." Then turned to her and said coolly, "Then we'll begin."

After he left, she peered around the room. The

table was filled with sharp things, but her chair was bolted to the floor. Other than that, and the chair that had housed Greenstone's big behind, nothing else was pliable.

The door opened, and a young Hispanic girl, probably fifteen, came in with a rag and bucket. With flared nostrils, she squatted to the mess. Laura frowned. So Greenstone was recruiting again. It was like all their work had been for nothing. It was enough to make Laura puke again.

"I'm Laura, what's your name?"

The girl ignored her and began cleaning.

"Look, you know I used to be you. Recruited by Greenstone at a young age. Taught to fight. Taught to kill."

Still silence.

"Someday you'll be me."

She stopped and looked at Laura, but said nothing.

"When he is tired of you, he will kill you. That is what he does. I was here for more than a decade. I saw a lot of bad stuff. Lots of my friends died."

"You're lying," she said, but didn't continue to scrub.

"I wish I were, kid." It took everything she had, but Laura managed to produce some tears.

"I'm not supposed to talk to you." She went back to scrubbing.

"You've been here, what, a month? I can tell by your uniform and the pleasant job they've given you."

"Three weeks."

"You don't want to die here. But you will."

She dropped the cloth in the bucket and walked out.

Laura sighed. She had pushed too hard.

To her surprise, the girl came back. She glanced down the hall, then walked back in. "Why do you keep saying that?"

"Because, like I said. I've seen it a million times." Laura tried to straighten. "What is your name?"

"Alicia."

"Well, Alicia, if you get me out of this, I will get you out of here. Back to your life, if you want, or you can stay with me. Your choice."

The girl tucked her black hair behind both ears, licked her lips, and nodded. It almost seemed too simple. But three weeks. She was still green. Not totally indoctrinated.

"You have to hurry though. We can't get caught."

Alicia grabbed one of the sharp tools off the table and slit the plastic bindings. Laura jumped to stand, but almost fell over from the drugs.

"I need your help. He gave me something."

"Okay." Alicia reached an arm around her and led her to the door. She peeked around and jumped back. "He's coming."

Perfect. A small smile crept on Laura's face. "Walk out like nothing is wrong. Meet me in the hall in a little bit."

Her expression appeared unsure, but she complied.

Laura grabbed a tool from the table and sat back in the chair just seconds before he walked in. She lifted her head, as if dazed and confused by his presence.

"Are you ready to begin?"

You have no idea. "Begin what exactly?"

"Torture, of course."

"To what end?"

He laughed. "Part for my enjoyment and the other part, because I need to know what you know."

He turned to the table. "Tell me, my dear, what do you know?"

"Tell me where my friends are first."

His fleshy frame turned with a raised eyebrow. "Your friends? You mean recruits, don't you?"

"Where are they?"

"If I told you, then I would be pontificating like they do in the movies. Then you'd break out somehow and rescue them. I can't have that." He walked toward her with a scalpel and held it by her nose. "Though I am sure you'd love to keep that pretty face of yours, it won't do you any good six feet under the ground."

Laura didn't hesitate. She plunged the tool deep into his neck and head butted him across the room. Greenstone flew against the wall, blood seeping out in spurts, spraying the room. She ran to the hall.

Alicia popped out from an open doorway. Her eyes scanned Laura's body and went wide.

Laura glanced down. Splatters of scarlet red covered her clothes. "It had to be done. Come on!"

She grabbed an old blanket on the way and tried to wipe as much of his blood from her face and hands as she could. Together, they ran down the hall of the old S.I.U. building to the far lot. Once out of the building, Laura pulled her the one place she knew there were no cameras. A place Bryce had once stolen a kiss. She faced Alicia. "Do you know where they are keeping my friends?"

Her head lowered, and she pointed to a metal hatch across the way.

Oh no, the pit.

Chapter Eight

Eri opened her eyes, but saw nothing but darkness. Water dripped from overhead. The stench in the air was rancid and strong. She touched the ground below her. The floor felt wet, cold, hard, and rough. Where was she? Where were her friends? "Charlie? Myers?"

Someone moaned next to her.

She inched forward and hit a body. "Charlie?"

"Nah. It's Myers." His hand touched hers.

She hugged him. "Where are we?"

"The pit," came Bryce's voice across the sea of pitch black. "I've been here before. Only not this far down."

Something crawled over her hand. She screamed.

"What's wrong?" Myers said.

"I felt something." Eri wiped down her arms and hands, then folded them into her body.

"Yeah, there are all sorts of dangerous wildlife down here. Fling it off if it is on you," Bryce said.

"Charlie?" she said again.

"Here," he said weakly on her other side.

She crawled to the voice. "Are you okay?"

His face felt damp, but warm. "I think I have a cut just above my eye."

"Yeah, I'm pretty banged up too," Myers said. "I think we were tossed in."

"It's too far down for that," Bryce said. "Curious

how they did it. But, I suppose, the bigger question is how do we get out?"

The top opened. The glow outlined a woman's head.

"Laura?" Bryce said.

"No. It's Helena."

Eri knew they couldn't trust her. The girl had smoked them out. But they would deal with that at the top. Eri grabbed hold of the rope and walked up the side of the cement cylinder, her biceps screaming with each foot. At the top, Helena offered a hand. Eri hesitated, but only for a moment. She pulled up and crawled away from the hold. Her friends joined her moments later. The moon was high. They needed to find cover. A breeze blew and the cuts and bites stung on her arms. She tried to block out the pain. No time for that now. "We need shelter."

"Where can we go?" Charlie asked.

"Back to my dad's house," Helen said.

Everyone swung to her in a fluid motion, each with clear disdain. "You're joking, right?" Eri flipped around Helena and placed her in a chokehold. One move, and the girl would die. "Start talking!"

A small squeak exited her mouth.

Eri lessened her restraint. "Again."

"They kidnapped my sister and then shot my father in front of me." She coughed. "I had no choice." Her eyes drifted to Bryce. "I lied when I said my father told me about Laura Black. They did. They told me she would come and if I wanted to see my sister again, then I needed to contact them and help execute their plan."

"What plan?" Eri spat.

"To lure Laura Black back to the compound. If you

hadn't suggested it, I was supposed to."

"Who?" She wiggled to free herself, but Eri held tight. "Who?"

"Greenstone."

The group all started murmuring at once. Greenstone was alive? None of them would feel safe now.

Bryce knelt next to her. "Did he pull the trigger?"

Helena shook her head. "No, there was another guy. He seemed to be in charge. I don't know his name though."

Bryce looked at Eri and nodded.

Eri let go.

The girl fell at her feet, gasping for air. "Thank you."

Eri rolled her eyes. "Please." She peered at the group. "So, what now? We're sitting ducks out here. We need to regroup and figure out where Laura is."

"We can go to my house. It is not far," Helena said again.

"Don't you think they'll come there?" Charlie replied. "Another trap?"

Helena shook her long black hair. "I don't think they know you're free."

Eri glanced at the tropical forest around them. The forest was dense, but she knew there were eyes everywhere on this property. "We need to get out of here before someone sees us. Let's go to the house."

Helena nodded and pointed north.

The group ran forward, not quick to avoid cover or a fast look around. They had all been here before. Other than the lack of guards trying to kill them, this escape was not new. Where was everyone? That worried Eri a bit, only because it seemed something was off. Were they all being led into another con? One that would kill all of them this time? But if that were so, why not let them all rot in the pit? None of it really made sense.

They rounded the gate and ran for the fields.

"Watch out for mines," Bryce yelled back.

Instantly, everyone slowed and checked their footing. The humidity in the air was thick and suffocating. Eri pulled off her hoodie and tied it around her waist. The breeze nipped at cuts and bites. They once again stung. It was too dark to assess the damage. Some itched, some hurt. Her lungs screamed for more air and her body for water. The trek must have been close to a half hour. The group was haggard from lack of sleep and food, as well as the damage done in the pit.

"It's to the left," Helena said, pointing.

The group halted and looked at the bamboo shack. They had been here before. She glanced at Helena. "Who is your dad?"

"Julio Peron."

Everything cleared. That was Laura's ally. "Let's go," Eri said.

Cautiously, they approached the front. Charlie opened the door. A puddle of blood and maggots lay just inside. The house smelt of day old garbage and death. Everyone audibly winced or gagged.

Eri willed herself not to vomit. "Why haven't you cleaned up?"

"We buried him out back," Helena said, as if that was enough.

"How do we stay here?" Charlie asked. "This place reeks."

"There is a hidden house in back. Remember, it is

where Bryce got better." Eri turned to Helena. "Can you show it to us?"

Helena nodded, took them through a room, and flipped on an overhead light that set off a green glow. A shelf flipped around, and the group entered what appeared to be a bunker. The room was just a bit bigger than a prison cell, but it would work for what they needed to do.

"I'll get you some food and water," Helena said.

"Myers, go with her," Bryce said.

He nodded and left behind the young woman.

Eri dropped to a cot on the floor. Charlie sat next to her. Bryce stayed by the doorway, noticeable worry on his face. Laura was missing. None of them spoke for a few minutes. They needed to catch their breath and collect their thoughts. How did they get here? Not one decision in the last week was the right one. They were smarter than this. Why had Laura brought them here? It was dangerous. Reckless. Anger rose in Eri's chest. She didn't understand the foolishness of this, and she just wanted to get out of here.

"Are you okay?" Charlie stared down at her arms.

Eri followed his gaze. Several large bites seemed to be swelling on her right arm. One looked to be infected. "I'm sure I'll be fine."

"We should do something about them." Charlie started to get up.

She grabbed his wrist and pulled him back down. "In time. First, we need to figure out a plan." Her gaze shifted to Bryce. "We need to get Laura back."

Bryce visibly inhaled and nodded.

"I'd like to know who we are fighting." Charlie laid his head against the wall and stared at the ceiling.

"The same jerks who tried to kill us a year ago."

Charlie's hand slightly touched hers. Electricity coursed through her system. She tried not to react, but Charlie noticed. He lifted his head and looked at her, knowingly.

Both looked back at Bryce. His eyes were closed.

Charlie ran his index finger down her hand.

She closed her eyes, wanting to kiss him. *So dumb to think of such a thing now.* Never had she felt so distracted. She opened her hand and allowed him to cup hers. Someone was coming. Quickly, she dropped her sweatshirt over the joined fingers.

Charlie smirked.

"What?"

"I think I love you," he whispered.

Her heart pounded. Of course, they loved each other. They were family. But she knew that wasn't what he meant. Bryce moved to the side as Helena and Myers entered with a plate of cheese and bread, as well as bottles of water.

Eri let go of Charlie's hand and reached for the water. Within seconds, she devoured it.

"Helena, do you have a first aid kit?" Charlie asked, as he replaced the cap on his empty bottle. "I think we are pretty banged up from the pit."

"Yeah, I think so." She walked out.

Myers turned to the room. "So, what is our big plan?"

Chapter Nine

Laura thought of the pit and the last time she had placed Bryce inside. It was a vile place filled with all sorts of scary creatures. Chances are they were left there to die. If the right thing bit them, they could. No time to waste. Laura grabbed Alicia's arm and ran with her through the jungle to the cement cellar. The hatch lay just ahead. It fell open like access on a submarine. Inside was darkness. Silence.

"Hello?" Laura yelled down.

It echoed, without response.

Laura looked at Alicia. "Are you sure?"

The girl nodded. "Positive. I saw him place them in."

Fear gripped Laura's heart. "Bryce?" She waited. "Eri? Charlie? Myers?"

No response. Laura sat to the ground, unsure what to do next. Where could they be?

"What if they got out?" Alicia asked.

"Unlikely. No one can escape the pit."

Alicia held up a rope in the grass next to the opening. "They could if they had help."

Laura grabbed the rope and glanced around. It had been tied off. Yes, it appeared they were rescued. She scanned the forest around them. But how long ago? And where would they go? Maybe she could track them. The sun slowly rose just below the tree line helping her to see more. The ground was damp enough to create a few footsteps. She sprinted after them. Alicia followed close behind. The trail led outside the gate and down a dirt path. They followed the route for close to half an hour.

"Where are you going, Bryce?" Laura whispered out loud.

"Did you say something?" Alicia panted behind her.

Laura shook her head.

"We are close to my home. We could go there."

"Your home?" Laura faced her.

"Yeah, my papa and sister are likely scared for me. Come on, I'll show you." They headed to the left and instantly it clicked. This was Julio's other daughter. Over the years, Julio had discussed his two daughters who lived with their mother. She had never met them. *Until now?*

"Was your dad Julio Peron?"

She stopped, eyes wide. "Yes. Do you know him?"

Oh no. The reality of what was about to happen made Laura sick. The girl did not know her father had been murdered. Did she tell her?

Laura hesitated as she remembered Helena's betrayal. Were both sisters working for Greenstone? Millions of question revolved around in her head. She didn't know what to do. The good news—she had a gun.

"What's wrong?" Alicia asked. "I promise. It isn't far."

Laura nodded, fully aware this could be a trap. "Lead the way."

****

The driveway came into view. Laura's antennas went up. Totally alert, she readied herself for anything. There was another truth that also plagued her. Did she really want this young girl to find out her father had been murdered in her home? They had buried the body, but they hadn't cleaned up the mess.

"Wait," Laura said.

Alicia stopped and faced her. "This is my house. It's okay. We can go in."

How did she share this news? Laura was used to being blunt, but the last year had softened her a bit. She bit her lip, inhaled deeply, and exhaled slowly. "Your father, he was…killed."

The girl stared her; the news obviously did not compute.

Laura opened her mouth to speak again, but stopped when movement happened in the doorway of the house. "Get down."

The two of them ducked behind a beat-up station wagon. Laura readied her gun. A figure came into view. *Bryce!*

Laura ran out from behind the car and jumped into his arms. Her heart hammered in her chest. She wrapped her legs around him and kissed him passionately. "I missed you," she whispered between kisses.

"I hadn't noticed." He laughed. "Ditto."

Alicia passed them, and Laura reached to grab her arm until she saw Helena. Instead, she prepared to shoot. Helena had betrayed them. No one betrayed her family.

Bryce touched the top of the gun and pushed. "She had a good reason."

"It better be, or I'll shoot her."

"Don't worry, I'll explain." Bryce cupped her chin and kissed her lightly on the lips. He did have a way with her heart that no one else did.

Helena and Alicia hugged and then cried as the news of their father was shared. Though angry with Helena, it had to be hard.

Bryce led them all back into the house and into the bunker. The room was filled wall-to-wall with people. Between the odor due to no showers for more than twenty-four hours, especially after running through the balmy jungle, and the lingering smell of putrefied blood in the other room—the air was a tad pungent. But they had been in worse situations. Everyone stared; no one talked. Each probably pondering the same thing as her.

Where did they to go next? What were they up against? Was Greenstone acting alone?

Helena had indicated there was someone else who had shot her father. Whoever that person was, was he in charge? Did that mean Greenstone was not the head of S.I.U. as she had assumed for years?

"We need to disappear," Charlie finally said, cutting the silence.

"We need to fight back." Myers stood and started one of his usual cursing tirades. All they could do was watch. Finally, he spun around the room and asked, "Aren't you all tired of this?"

"Yeah, of course." Charlie stood facing him. "We all are, man. But if we do not mend and plan, we will just be back to this place again…or worse, end up shot. We need time. We need to hide somewhere and get our act together."

Laura had to agree with Charlie. Though she

wanted desperately to stick it to any remnants of S.I.U., she also knew they needed time. "We will do both. Charlie is right, we need to heal, get stronger, and develop a strategy. This jumping at them without real intel is killing us."

Myers winced.

Bad choice of words. "Sorry." Laura bit her lip, trying to think of something else to say. She slid off the trunk she was on to the cement floor. "The question is where can we go? Any place I know will be compromised. I need something out of the way that isn't directly connected to anyone."

Charlie glanced at Eri and then back to Laura. "Eri knows people in Chinatown that can make people disappear."

Laura looked at Eri. "Is that true?"

She nodded. "Yes, assuming my being dead doesn't complicate things."

"It's worth a shot." Laura grabbed a cracker from the tray on the floor, broke off a small piece, and tossed it in her mouth. "What's the worst that can happen?"

Bryce and Charlie laughed.

"I would like to come with you." Helena stood. "We can't stay here, and we are now hunted too."

A flash memory of Helena placing that mask on her face sent an injection of rage through her system. Laura shook her head. "Absolutely not."

"I explained to you why I did what I did. I am sorry, but I'm not a spy. I just wanted my sister back." Helena tried to touch Laura, but she recoiled. No way was this girl to be trusted. *Fool me once, fool me twice...*

A quick glance around the room indicated the

group might not share her fear. Each expression seemed to plead with her to consider this request. Didn't they understand? "Look, Helena, we can't trust you. How do we know this isn't some sort of long game?"

Helena furrowed her brow. "Long what?"

"Nice." Laura shook her head, stood, pushed the gun into the waistband of her jeans, and exited the claustrophobic quarters before she did something she might regret.

She stormed through the living room and onto the porch. Though the air hung heavy and warm, it felt fresh and relaxing.

Bryce came behind her and wrapped his arm around her waist. "You can't leave her."

"Watch me!" She stepped away from him, staring out into the jungle.

His face came into view as he circled her, his intense blue eyes still made her swoon. "Laura, please. Leaving them here is a death sentence, and you know it."

"We can't trust her."

He kissed her cheek. Her nose. Lips. Soft, tempting, even now. "We can stick Myers on her as a baby sitter. If anyone needs a job, it's him. He will not leave her side, and he's dying for payback. One wrong move, he'll deal with her. No doubt."

She considered this. That was a good solution and could keep Myers from running off to ruin things. "Okay, I like that."

Their lips met again. "I like you," he whispered.

"Then marry me." She smirked.

He laughed. "As soon as we find a minister, done."

"I'm ordained," Charlie said from the doorway.

"Anyone can get ordained on the Internet."

Both of them turned to see him and laughed.

"As soon as we can breathe, I might just take you up on that," Bryce said.

"We definitely can't breathe here." Charlie slammed the screen door closed, holding his nose. "Can we go now?"

Laura giggled. Something she didn't do. It occurred to her what just happened. Was she engaged? Tough girl or not, she was still a girl. And inside, the idea of marrying Bryce filled her with true emotions of love.

"Yes, we can leave." She turned to Bryce. "And not that you really asked me yet, but yes, I will marry you…well, as soon as it is right."

He bent down on one knee.

Laura smiled.

"Will you marry me?"

She playfully slapped his shoulder. "I just said I would."

"You said I didn't ask you. So, now I'm properly asking."

"Yes, crazy person, I will happily marry you."

The group hollered from the doorway.

Laura and Bryce turned and laughed.

Everyone piled around them, hugging them.

"Mom and Dad are getting married," Charlie said jokingly.

Laura shook her head. "Okay, enough. For now, let's just get out of country."

"Agreed," Bryce said, squeezing her hand.

Everyone nodded in agreement.

Chapter Ten

Eri's heart pounded in her ears. This was hopefully smart, and not idiotic, to bring them all here. This entire community had mourned her death. Greenstone would have made sure of it. Would they believe it was her? Millions of emotions and questions spiraled through her mind. In the midst of that, however, she felt a sense of nostalgia as they passed through the brightly colored streets of Chinatown. Strong smells of teriyaki, roasted duck, and cooked vegetables filtered through the air. Sounds of her native tongue surrounded her. People drove by on rickshaws and motorbikes. Hundreds of people lined the streets, hurried to their next destination. It felt surreal, but wonderful to be home.

"In here." Eri pointed to the gold entrance marked with the painted black words, *Wan Ju Lee's Judo Dojo*. It wasn't where she trained, but Laura had said to avoid anything too close. The sensei could connect her to Jane Chu, an old friend she could trust.

A small lobby filled with rice paper walls and long, white and black banners with inscriptions that read in Hànzì letters, *Honor*, *Balance*, and *Gentle*. A few dark wooden benches lined the entrance. Eri motioned for them to sit. Her hair stood on end, and her heartbeat raced like a rabbit on steroids. Every pore in her body said this was not a good play. Was she paranoid or wise? Silently, she prayed this was not the dumbest thing she had ever done.

An elderly Chinese lady dressed in a kimono and slippers entered and bowed. She spoke in Mandarin to Eri. "Can I help you?"

Eri responded in the same language. "I need to speak to Jane Chu."

"Jane Chu does not compete in this dojo."

Eri nodded. "Yes, but I cannot go there. Can you contact her and ask her to meet us here? Tell her Eri Lee Young is alive and in need of assistance."

The woman's eyes grew wide. She must have remembered her name. Her uncle had been a well-respected master in the area. "Are you in trouble?"

"Yes."

The women's gaze danced around the room, directed at her friends. She probably wondered if they were with or against her. They held blank, but slightly expectant expressions, unaware of what was transpiring.

"These are my friends," Eri explained.

"One moment, please." The women bowed and then scuffled away behind a wall of black beads.

Eri turned to the group. "Now we wait."

"What was the conversation?" Charlie asked.

She shrugged. "Basically, I asked her to find my friend and bring her here. I hope no one gets tipped off. This town can be very tricky. One minute, you think you have an ally. The next, you realize you do not."

"And this Jane Chu? You can trust her?" Laura asked.

Eri raised an eyebrow. "You understood us?"

A small smiled tugged at the corner of Laura's mouth. "I can speak most of the main languages of the world. I had to learn one every year I was in S.I.U."

Bryce leaned over and kissed her head. "Just when I didn't think you could impress me more."

"That is not common knowledge, however, I prefer for people to assume I do not understand. They always show their cards that way."

Everyone nodded.

The woman returned and spoke to Eri. "She will meet you in back. This way."

The group walked through the beads, past a class of young students sparring, to an empty practice room. The woman waved for them to wait and left.

A loud scream came from the far wall. Jane Chu jumped out from behind a rice paper partition and punched her in the chest. Eri fell to the mat.

Charlie and Laura jumped in, ready to fight.

"No, stop! This Jane. It will be me and her." Eri took a fighting stance. "She needs to know it is me."

Jane swung.

Eri blocked.

With another scream, Jane kicked at Eri's head. Eri ducked just in time. She skated into a leg-sweep. Jane fell to the mat, but popped back up. Hit. Block. Hit. Block. The two stepped around the mat. Jane kicked again, hitting her stomach. Winded, Eri fell but managed to roll backward to her feet.

"She's hurt," she heard Charlie say.

Eri labored to block him out. With the palm of her hand, she hit Jane in the jaw. Rather than swing again, Jane stepped back, bowed, and ran to hug her. The words that flew from Jane's lips were so fast and the emotion so overwhelming Eri couldn't understand what her friend was saying. Finally, she made out, "It is you.

You're alive."

Eri pulled from her grasp and smiled. "I am, my good friend." Jane was a little heavier and older, but she still held the sweet smile from their youth. "They kidnapped me and faked my death. We escaped, but not without trouble."

Jane glanced at her friends on the word *we*. "They are with you?"

"Yes. I could not have made it without them. They are my family."

Jane waved for them to follow. Outside the room was a small table with eight pillows on the floor. The walls were bare, with only a few small windows high on the wall to shed light. The floor was clay with a drainage grate in the center. *A place for blood to empty?* She didn't know she could be this scared. It reminded her of a jail cell she had once visited in China. Her eyes glanced around for exits. Other than how they had entered, there were none. *Not good.*

Jane motioned for them to sit. "I will get some tea, and we can talk."

The team sat. Did they all feel the same apprehension in their stomachs Eri did? They did not know Jane. They only knew Eri and trusted her. But how many times before had they felt betrayed? This room only amplified that feeling. The only solace was Jane did not close the door when she left.

"Should we be worried?" Charlie asked in a hushed tone.

Eri held a finger to her lips.

Jane entered with a pot of tea and a plate of cookies and rice crackers. "Now, how can I help?"

"We are running from the people who took me."

Eri poured herself some tea and faced her friend. "Right now, we just need a place to lay low. A place where no one would come looking for us." She secured eyes with Jane in order to read her. "Uncle had talked about such places before. Do you know of any?"

The young woman before her seemed more poised than ever before. Though they spent their childhood sparing, Eri had always been the more subdued one. Though three years older than Eri, Jane was usually more wild and mischievous. She typically made jokes or got the two of them in trouble. To see her friend so relaxed worried her. She sipped from the teacup and then nodded to the plate. There were several almond cookies and just one fortune cookie on the plate. Strange, since Jane didn't normally serve them. "May you achieve good fortune."

Eri glanced at Laura and then to the plate. She reached for it; everyone visibly leaned in. With a snap, she cracked it open and began to read the handwritten note inside: *This cookie was made just in case. They are watching. You must go and never come back.*

Jane sipped again. "I wish I could be more help. But I do not really have any place in mind."

Eri stood and, with a panicked expression, made sure to look into every eye, indicating her fear. "I understand."

Jane rose with grace. "Leaving so soon?"

"Well, we don't want to get stuck in LA traffic, do we?" Eri hugged her neck and felt something slide into her pocket.

"It is so good to see you. You'll have to come back again for more cookies and tea," Jane said coolly.

Eri nodded, wiping at the tears welling in her eyes.

This would be the last time she would ever see her friend. "Yes, of course. Goodbye."

The mass scrambled to the door, down through the hall, and to the front lobby. The elderly woman waited there with a paper bag. "Leftovers for your journey."

Eri smiled, bowed, and exited with her crew in tow. Once on the street, she hurried through the crowd, only peering back to see they were following close behind. There was definitely concern on their faces, but she didn't have time to explain. No surprise, they were in danger. If they were watching Jane, there could be a tap on her phone intercepted when the elderly woman had called her. She could have a tail that followed her to the place. Many ideas were circling in Eri's head. They had to disappear—now.

Luckily, Eri had grown up here. The streets were second nature. People all around her laughed and spoke in several dialects. Her eyes darted from person to person, hoping none of them noticed her. At the end of the street, she ducked into an alley. The crew, behind her, followed suit. Above was a ladder. She yanked on it. Nothing. Charlie reached up with her and yanked. Still nothing.

"Move," Myers said.

They shuffled back.

Myers yanked, and it squeaked to the ground. He really was the brawn. They began climbing when two men came around the corner straight for them.

"They can't know we're here," Eri whispered down the ladder. "Laura, we'll have to take them out." She climbed back down and joined Laura on the ground. Myers and Charlie stood behind them. Helena and Alicia hid against the wall.

One man clicked opened a knife; the other produced a nunchaku.

Eri reached in the bag from Jane and produced a pistol. "Never bring a knife to a gun fight boys." She fired twice, dropping both to the ground.

Alicia screamed.

Myers grabbed her and covered her mouth. "Silence, baby girl, or you'll get us all killed."

"But you shot them." Alicia sniffed. "Did you have to shoot them?"

Laura stepped to the sides of the bodies. "Myers and Eri, get the girls up the ladder. Charlie and Bryce, help me get rid of the bodies."

Eri grabbed Helena by the arm and pushed her toward the ladder. Myers did the same with Alicia. The four of them rose to the third floor. Eri glanced back down. The rest of them were gone. She turned back to a grate at the top. It had been ten years since she had been here. *Please don't let anyone be inside.* She slid the vent covering to the landing and motioned for the three of them to climb in. "Myers, go in and look around to confirm it's safe. Girls, wait just inside. I'll stay here for the rest of our group."

They climbed through the dark hole and disappeared from sight. A muffled whimper could be heard. They never should have brought Alicia. She was too young and untrained. How long until she compromised them all?

Charlie came into view. Bryce and Laura jogged right behind him. They climbed the ladder and into the hole. Eri grabbed the grate, climbed in, and closed them in. The room was dark, and she couldn't see where everyone was positioned.

"Anyone have a light?" She reached into the bag, hopeful. Most things felt warm and soft like food. But something small rattled in her hand. *Matches?* She frowned. Of course, Jane would give her matches instead of a flashlight. She lit one, and the soft glow revealed everyone sitting among piles of cardboard boxes and metal trunks. It hadn't changed from when she was a kid. The attic was still a place of mystery, and the perfect place for them to hide. The match burned to her fingers, forcing her to let it go. With a quick strike, she lit another. "Myers, there should be a box of candles just past your foot."

He reached for it and dug inside. Within seconds, he produced a metal jar. He rolled it to her and she lit it.

"How do you know about this place?" Laura's eyes narrowed. "Is it too close to you? Will people come looking for you here?"

Eri shook her head. "No one knew about this place. It was my secret hideout when my aunt would yell at me. I found it by accident one day. There was this bird I was following. It went inside. I went with it." Eri sat the candle in the middle of the room and crossed next to Charlie who sat on a pile of blankets. "I don't know who owns the house, but they are always gone this time of year. Everything is still the way it was a decade ago."

Laura didn't seem convinced, but she nodded. "We all need sleep. Did your friend give you any water in that bag?"

"In fact, she did. And some baozi to eat." She took a sip of water and then passed it. Everyone took a sip. When it reached Alicia, the girl refused to drink. Tears streamed down her face, her body trembled. Helena held her, petting her head. Eri sighed. Why did they bring her?

"Are you okay?" she said more annoyed than caring.

Alicia shook her head.

"Laura, we shouldn't have brought them. They will only slow us down," Eri said.

"Eri," Myers snapped.

"What? It's true. Look at her." Eri waved a hand in her direction. "I'm not being cruel, I'm being honest."

Helen's eyes met hers. "I know you think we are not well trained, but our father did more to ready us than you think. We can speak three languages, fire a hand gun, and know Xilam."

"Xilam?" Charlie whispered.

"Mexican martial arts," Laura said back.

Helena's voice rose in irritation. "My sister doesn't cry because she is scared. She cries, because seeing another man shot gave her vision of how our father died."

A shot of guilt resounded in Eri's chest. *Of course.* She just assumed. But that made sense. "I'm sorry."

"We will not get in your way, and we can keep up." Helena kneeled to her sister's side and pulled Alicia's head to her shoulder.

"Okay," Eri said.

Myers wiped his eyes. This had to be hard for him, too. Far too much death surrounded them.

Exhaustion finally caught up with Eri's body. Every bone and muscle felt fatigued. She lay back on the blanket and closed her eyes. It had been a while since rested sleep would come. But before another thought entered her mind, she was out.

Chapter Eleven

Laura slowly opened her eyes. Light streamed through the outside grate and the boards of the attic. Snoring, especially from Myers, echoed cadence in the room. Through slits of heavy eyelids, she peered at her sleeping family and sighed. She could not seem to keep them safe. Why did she keep making foolish choices? It wasn't like her to be rash and uncontrolled. Emotions had made her soft and reckless. Bryce found it enduring. She deemed it weak, a frailty that could get them all killed. She laid her cheek on Bryce's chest and closed her eyes. What were they going to do?

"Good morning," she heard Charlie whisper a few feet away.

Laura peeked through one eye just in time to see Charlie kiss Eri on the forehead and lips. Maybe she was still asleep. It would be absurd that the two of them were together? Nothing about that couple made sense. But then, did she and Bryce really make sense either?

Bryce squirmed under her, and she lifted her head.

"Hi," he said softly.

"Hi," she rasped back.

Charlie sat up, yawning. "What I wouldn't do for even half a cup of Bryce's sludge coffee about now."

Bryce laughed, sitting up against the slanted wall. "Hey, can I help it the Army taught me to make it strong?"

"Strong is an understatement. That stuff could lift Myers up and toss him." Charlie winked.

Myers lifted his head, eyes half-mast, pained expression on his face, clearly not awake yet. "Did someone say something?"

"Go back to sleep. The boys are just being stupid," Laura said.

Myers dropped back down and in seconds, his lurid rhythmic breathing resumed.

Laura tilted her neck side-to-side in a vain effort to work out the kinks from sleeping on a wooden floor. The air was crisp, causing vapor to form smoke as she breathed out. She pulled an old fur coat to her neck and cuddled back.

Bryce must have noticed. He placed his hands on her arms and rubbed. "It's chilly."

She nodded.

"I'm hungry." Charlie began rummaging in the bag from the night before. "Well, Eri has some weird looking dough balls in the bag here for everyone to eat."

Eri sat up and smiled. "Baozi."

"Bonzi!" Charlie threw a fist in the air. "To baby trees."

Eri smacked him.

"What? *Karate Kid* was a great movie."

"It's baozi," Eri said.

"Or dough balls." Charlie winked.

"Baozi," Eri said a bit annoyed, though there was an element of playfulness in her stern tone.

Charlie sang, "You say baozi, I say dough balls. I guess we better call the whole thing off."

Eri shot him a warning look.

Laura was likely the only one who caught it. "Well, I'm starved. Just tell me what it is, and I'm ready to eat it."

"Baozi is a steamed bun. Usually, there is some kind of meat or vegetable inside." Eri pulled out a wooden box and passed it around. "Everyone take one."

Laura lifted the baseball size white ball out of the box and passed the container to Bryce to do the same.

Myers sat up just in time to take one and pass it on.

The texture was soft, and the flavor inside was savory. It hit the spot. She swallowed her last bit with a swig of water from a water bottle and then turned to the room. "We need to talk strategy. This is obviously not some place we can stay another day. There are people here looking for us. We need a longer term plan."

The expressions spoke volumes. They were tired and confused. No one had an answer. Where could they hide? S.I.U. had eyes everywhere. It was obvious everyone was wearing thin. They needed to regroup. *But where?*

"What about we head for some remote place? Something totally off the grid?" Charlie said.

"Yeah, but where?" Laura echoed her thoughts.

Together, collectively, they all seemed to ponder that for quite a while.

"What about this?" Myers sat forward. "When I was really little, my family used to go to Lake Tahoe for different vacations. It was completely off the beaten path and lots of places to hide. With snow coming, if we get in, people will not be able to get to us for a while. It will give us time to plan, get healthy, and be ready to fight this spring."

"And we could live off the land. I like it," Bryce

said.

Nodding, Myers bit into the dough ball.

Laura was surprised Myers was willing to wait that long. "You're okay delaying your desire to get even?"

"I don't want to see anyone else die," his voice cracked. "We need to get our heads on straight. Me, especially."

"Lake Tahoe, huh?" Laura smiled and glanced at Bryce.

He winked.

The group all shared different thoughts about the plan, all of them positive.

"Then it's settled." Laura rubbed her hands together. "We leave at after sunset."

****

Laura reached into another cardboard box and pulled out some photo albums and a shoebox filled with letters. Others in the room had had more luck. Charlie found a couple of knives. Eri found cases of Army food, as well as, some clothes for them to change into. Julio's kids unearthed maps of the city. Laura frowned at her contents and then dropped the memories back in the box, coughing at the cloud of dust that followed. She slid the box out of the way. A trunk sat to her left. She opted for that one first. She pushed on a button next to the lock, but it didn't budge. "Myers, come pick this lock."

He smiled. "Just a second." He grabbed a few things in his pile of goodies and shuffled on his knees to her position. Bending down, he withdrew a couple of bobby pins and knife. It took a few seconds, but he was able to jiggle it open. The lid popped up, and each of them leaned in. *Gold mine!*

"Eureka," Charlie exclaimed.

"My thoughts exactly, kid," Bryce said.

Inside were a bunch of antique guns and rifles. Each, surprisingly, appeared polished and new. The caretaker of these deemed them important. She suspected this robbery would likely hurt the most.

"Will they fire?" Charlie asked.

Laura lifted a Remington Rollback into her hands and marveled at its beauty. She knew guns. This was easily late 1800s. "They'll fire, but no guarantees out which end."

"In other words, you could blow your face off," Eri said, pulling a Colt Davis from the box.

Several boxes of shells and cartridges sat to the side of them. They may need them. It was a risk they may have to take. "I say we take it all. It could come in handy. When we make it to the forest, we'll find some safe way to test them. If nothing else, it will help us get dinner out in the middle of nowhere."

Bryce drooled over the Winchester in his hand.

"Want to trade?" Charlie said, holding up a small Colt pistol.

"Not likely," Bryce said.

The room began to grow dark. Laura glanced at her watch. *5:42 p.m. Almost sunset.* "It's time."

Each person loaded their bounty into different bags they had found. Myers and Charlie slipped out with their usual mission to find a car. Once they returned, the group would set off.

The girls chatted in Spanish and giggled to her right.

Something rumbled below. Laura held up hand. "Sshh!"

Everyone froze.

Footsteps, several pairs, doors slamming—someone was home beneath them. Laura glanced at Eri.

Eri's eyes were wide with surprise. "They never come home this time of year," she hissed.

"We have to go." Laura started carefully collecting their bags.

"But Charlie and Myers?" Eri asked.

"We'll meet them below." Shuffling forward, as quick as they could without making noise, they crawled to the grate. Eri removed it and one-by-one, each of them stepped out onto the ladder.

"Hey! What are you doing up there?" a voice yelled from below.

Laura peered down. A moving van sat at the back entrance, and a young guy stood behind it looking at them. "No time, go! Go!"

They tore down the ladder, but the man reached the bottom. Now what?

"Whatever you took, hand it over!" The guy was not the owner. He couldn't be more than twenty-five. A son, maybe?

"You don't live here," Eri said with more confidence than she felt. "Why should we?"

"My dad passed away. I'm picking up his stuff. Now hand it over."

Laura glanced at Eri.

Eri nodded and placed the burlap sack behind her, then crouched, ready to fight.

"Keep going girls," Laura said over her shoulder to Helena and Alicia.

"I'm calling the cops," the guy said.

Eri round kicked the cell phone from his hand,

sending it under a dumpster a few feet away. The man looked startled. "I suggest you just stand there until all my friends are on the ground."

The three of them walked next to Eri. She leaned to Laura's ear. "Do we take the truck?"

Laura shook her head. "GPS."

A beige SUV pulled in the lot with Charlie at the helm.

"That's our ride." Laura grabbed the two girls and pushed them in.

The man went for his phone.

Eri jumped in the back. "Go!"

"Now we'll have to ditch this car, too." Laura hit the seat with her fist. "Shoot!"

Bryce touched her hand. "It's fine."

Myers pointed to a used car lot a few feet away. "I've got an idea. Do we still have some of those fake IDs?"

"Yeah, I keep them in my boot. Greenstone didn't find them." Laura unzipped her combat boot and lifted the lining of the shoe.

"So that's why you seem so tall," Charlie kidded, as he pulled over.

She lifted passports out and flipped through until she landed on a few of Myers'. "How about Albert Watson from Kentucky?"

Charlie laughed. "Go get 'em, cowboy."

"Now I need a cowboy hat." He reached for the plaid shirt on the back of Charlie's seat. "Sorry, man, need to borrow this thanks to Laura's creative imagination."

He stepped out of the van, threw the shirt on, pulled his pants over his boots, probably so that he looked less militaristic, and more hick.

"You could be a home terrorist, you know, the kind who supports the rebel flag," Charlie snickered.

Myers cursed at him and started across the street. Everyone leaned over the seats and watched as their friend made his way to the lot. In perfect theatrics, he pretended to be a customer in search of the perfect vehicle.

"Man, I wish I could hear this." Charlie rolled down the window in some vain effort. "We have got to get coms."

A balding man in a light blue shirt and navy tie approached Myers, arms wide, huge grin. The stereotype could not have been better written. They shook hands. Myers scanned the lot with his hand on his chin. Finally, he pointed to a car probably no one would miss—an old 70s Chevy van.

"Great, we just got rid of one of those," Eri said.

"Nah, it's The Agent Apparatus." Charlie put his hand on her shoulder and grinned. "It's our Mystery Machine."

"Our what?" Eri looked confused, which made Laura laugh.

"From *Scooby Doo*," Charlie said.

"Scooby who?"

Charlie's mouth dropped open. He looked at Laura for support.

She shrugged and smiled.

"I don't know if we can be friends anymore." Charlie shook his head and gazed back to the car dealership.

Eri swatted him and then followed his gaze.

Myers was behind the wheel, driving out of the lot.

Charlie started the engine and followed behind. About a mile away, they pulled over and everyone jumped from the SUV to get into their new Agent Apparatus. Myers approached them.

"No, that's not the plan. I'm going to go copy the key. We'll come take it when the place closes in a few hours. I looked around. Other than that chain, the lot seems pretty easy. Charlie, I'll need you to tap into any security cameras."

"We still need to ditch this car. It has to have a GPS on it, and that guy surely got the license plate," Eri said.

"Abandon it a few blocks from here." Laura pointed to an old rundown trucker's eatery across the street. "We'll go hang out at that diner until closing. This way, we'll know when we have the green light."

Chapter Twelve

Myers laughed at his performance. He stood in the lot, pretending he was unsure which vehicle to buy. When the salesman approached, Myers pretended he had a ton of his daddy's money to spend. The man, who introduced himself as Billy, was over the moon with joy. The guy was colorful and strange, which played to Myer's plan. When Myers pointed to the brown and gold van, Billy's face dropped. He probably would have liked to sell the Mercedes next to it. No bother. Myers was actually doing the man a favor. Billy would only lose about a thousand dollars tonight. That made Myers feel a tad better, and there was no GPS on an old vehicle like this one.

He glanced around the interior of the van. There was an orange and plaid cushioned bench on the side facing the door, a similar bench at the back, brown and gold shag carpet, wood paneling, and what looked like a kitchenette on the side by the door. This was perfect. Even if they couldn't find a place to stay, they could at least eat and sleep here.

Myers drove into a kiosk for making keys. Within a few minutes, he had his own set. He drove back to the lot and dropped the van off with Billy.

"So, shall we sign some papers?" Billy asked with a huge smile.

Myers shook his head. "I didn't like the way it

pulled to the left. I think I'll keep looking."

"You know we have other cars—"

"Nah, man, I really have my heart set on an older van. My pop used to have one, and well, it would just make me feel right having one, too." Myers stepped forward and put out his hand. "How about I get your card, and if I can't find a better one in a few days, maybe I'll come back."

Billy kept his mouth smiling, but his eyes shared disappointment. He handed out the card.

"Thank you, kindly." Myers smiled and crossed the street to the diner to meet the group. They sat in a back orange booth nursing sodas. "We're in business. Now we just need the shop to close."

They ordered, ate slow, talked a lot—but most of it Myers didn't hear. He couldn't help it. Now a days, flashes of Denise kept him sane. He just concentrated on her face—her smile and beautiful blue eyes. No way could he forget. If he just thought about it, maybe she didn't really leave him. But helping with tasks like this also helped greatly. They distracted him from the depression that was sure to take hold of him once denial turned into anger. He took a psychology class in high school and knew that was next. Getting away to a secluded spot before it took hold of him would be good. Without a doubt, it would hit hard. He needed to be trapped in Lake Tahoe snow when it did.

"The lights just went out," Laura said. "Charlie, log in."

Charlie pulled out his laptop and began hacking the security cameras. He held a thumb in the air. "We're golden."

"Let's move." Myers grabbed his stuff and went to

the exit.

Earlier Bryce had noticed a pair of bolt cutters in a storage shed behind the restaurant. He snatched them and jogged to the metal chain. He worked on it, while Myers unlocked the door to the van. He cranked it, and it purred to life. His eyes fell to Bryce. "Come on, man." It seemed to take Bryce several times, but eventually, the links snapped and he was able to roll the chain out of the way. Myers wasted no time. He gunned it. The group ran to the parking lot. Charlie ran to the driver's side. Myers jumped in back to open the door. Everyone piled in and slammed the door closed.

Charlie floored it. The entire adventure couldn't have taken more than five minutes. For a tiny second, Myers felt alive—able to block out the demons. He laid his head on the window behind his head and sighed.

They drove for a few hours, when they decided to change drivers. Without stopping, Bryce took the next shift and Charlie climbed to the back.

"Wow! This is pretty swank." Charlie lay on the carpet between them and made a slight snow angel in the shag. "I could get used to this."

"And you have no idea how many people have had a 'good time' on that floor," Eri said in disgust.

Charlie leapt up and onto one of the benches. "Gross."

Everyone laughed.

Laura leaned over to Myers and whispered, "I know you're not one for babysitting duty, but when we get to this hideout, you have to make sure the girls are not alone. They can't be making any calls or drops, if you know what I mean? I do not trust them yet."

He nodded.

Alicia and Helena rested across from him. Both were beautiful Hispanic women, who seemed to be kind-hearted, with a good sense of humor. But Laura was smart not to trust them. Each of them had a black mark to this group. The two of them would be the perfect Trojan horse. This task did not bother him. Once again, any job was a distraction.

****

They drove all night. Myers was the last to drive. Beams of light began to rake over the mountains, casting orange and purple hues. The round sphere seeped above the lowest peak, revealing snow and the lake below. The water sparked deep blue and the nature around them was glorious. Though Myers had been a mostly inside guy in his former life, he had always appreciated God's creation at its finest.

A dirt road lay just ahead. For some reason, he remembered it. He veered off, hoping it would be a good place to venture.

Laura leaned over his shoulder. "We need to make sure we stop at a general store or something before we get too deep. We'll need a few supplies."

"Do we have the money?" he asked.

"We have enough. Julio's girls grabbed their dad's stash and offered it up in exchange for bringing them."

Interesting. "Okay, I think I see one a few blocks ahead. Wake everyone."

Laura scooted back. Within seconds, sounds of everyone yawning and stretching could be heard throughout the van.

Myers glanced at Helena who snoozed in the passenger's seat. He tapped her. "Helena. We're going to stop at the General Store to get some supplies."

She rubbed her eyes and straightened in the seat. "How long was I asleep?"

"About two hours," Myers said. "We just entered Lake Tahoe about ten minutes ago."

Her head pivoted back and forth. "Wow, this is *muy bonita*, no? I like it."

He smiled. "Yes, it's very beautiful." Signaling to the left, Myers pulled off into the dirt lot. A log building sat in front of them with a sign that simply read, "Miguel's Outpost."

"Come on, everyone. Let's get what we need to last a few weeks up in the mountains." Laura slid the door open and stepped out onto the ground. The rest piled past her.

Myers got out the driver's side and joined them around the other side. The air was cool and fresh and smelled of pine. On the porch, he noticed a pay phone. He would need to stay close to Helena. She was his mission, and he planned to do it well. The last thing they needed was this girl making a phone call and putting them all in jeopardy.

"Get canned goods. Nothing perishable unless it has seeds," Laura ordered. "Lots of water, and some supplies we didn't get in the attic."

The outpost was surprisingly well stocked. The shelves were lined with groceries, as well as tourist paraphernalia. Helena and Alicia gravitated to a row of turquoise jewelry. Myers decided to focus on a few knives inches from them. Though he should be grabbing supplies, he needed to keep an eye on them.

Helena came next to him. "What did you find?"

"Some knives."

"Do you like any of them?"

He peered through the case and pointed to a sharp hunting knife with a koa carved hilt. "That's pretty cool."

"You should get it." She grinned at him, revealing a small dimple on her left cheek.

"We have more important stuff to take care of, and we have a knife."

"Myers," Laura said a few feet away. "Can you grab two bags of charcoal and lighter fluid?"

He nodded and walked to where they sat in back. When he returned, Laura spoke with drippy wet sweetness to the elderly gentleman behind the counter. That meant one thing. She was after something. "I don't suppose you know of any vacant cabins around here we could possibly rent for a while?"

"Oh, it's too bad you weren't here last week." The clerk rang another of her items and turned back. "The Jameson's own a cabin that they rent out during the holidays and were looking for someone. But I guess they gave up and left for Florida. They have a house there and won't probably be back until things heat up again." He held up a bottle of water. "If you'd like, I can give you a discount on these."

"Sure. Um, do you think I could get their contact information in Florida?"

Bagging the groceries, and not really looking at her, he said, "I don't. I'm sorry."

"But you know where they live?"

"Oh yes." He smiled. "Up there on Rondal Avenue. You know, you could maybe send them a postcard to their house. All their mail is forwarded." He pointed to a rack filled with colorful cards.

Myers lifted a bag of charcoal on the counter,

trying not to smile. The man had fallen hard into the spider's trap.

"What a wonderful idea." Laura crossed to the rack and pulled out a card displaying the blue lake with snowcapped mountains behind it. "I'll take this and a stamp if you have one."

"Sure do."

"One more thing. Any chance you would want to trade some antique guns for some of these?" She tapped on the glass covering guns.

The man leaned over, removed his glasses, and then glared at her in the eye. Myers prepared for anything.

"What you got?" the man said.

Laura smiled. "Myers, bring them in."

When Myers returned with three of the antique guns, he glanced back over to where he had left the girls. He didn't see Helena.

His heart raced. He set the guns down and walked to the door. *Oh no.* He strode to the exit and peered out. No one. He stepped back in and glanced around the store. His body relaxed. She was at another counter receiving a paper bag from a woman teller. Nervously, he smiled as she walked toward him, trying to calm the emotions he felt. "All done?"

"Yep." She grinned.

They both exited, and Myers joined them. Within a few minutes, the rest of the crew was also there. Quickly, they collected and loaded their supplies into the van. Myers got behind the wheel. "So, Rondal Street?"

"Avenue. And yes," Laura said, slamming the door closed.

They drove down the road in silence, ready to find their next temporary home.

Chapter Thirteen

Laura glanced over Myers' shoulder to see the cabin. It wasn't big, but it would do. "Everyone out. Be guarded until we know it is empty." She walked up the four wooden steps to a screen door. Reaching behind her back, she placed her right hand on her new Smith and Wesson, and then lifted her left hand to knock. Nothing. She knocked again. No answer. Slowly, she opened the screen door and tried the handle. It didn't budge.

Charlie walked next to her, ready to pick it.

She shook her head and lifted the mat. Empty. To her left was a strange ceramic mushroom that seemed out of place. Sure enough, inside was a key. She lifted it high and then placed it into the lock. It clicked. A chill swept through her as they entered. "We'll need to start a fire ASAP. I am betting it gets pretty cold here at night."

"Wow, this is beautiful," Eri said.

The ceiling was high with a balcony and doors on each side of the square space. Laura assumed that was where the bedrooms must be. In the center were a couch and several chairs. On the side facing away from the door was a large stone fireplace adorned with a real deer's head. The floor was wooden, covered only partially by a fur pelt. To the far end of the room was a table with long benches and a door. Laura walked through the door. It housed a small kitchenette and a staircase. She climbed it. It came out onto a balcony that led to several rooms. She peeked in each one. All three entries housed a bed. Where was the bathroom? She walked back down the steps and outside. Another small shack lay a few feet from the house. She peeked inside. It held a toilet, sink, and stand-up shower. "Well, that must be fun when it's twenty below."

Bryce came up behind her and slid his arm around her shoulders. His lips touched her cheek, and he pulled her around to face him. Their lips met soft and sweet. "This place should be good. How long do we have here?"

"They said until it warms, so I'm guessing a few months."

He pushed back a hair from her eyes. "My only concern is how warm we'll be. I hear it gets pretty cold, and other than the blankets we stole from the attic, we don't have much in the way of warmth."

"We'll need to collect lots of wood. What concerns me is this bathroom. Why did they put it so far from the house?"

His eyes scanned the small wooden shack. "Well, my guess is because they are not here during the winter. It was probably an outhouse at one point and time."

"Well it's dumb."

"Duly noted." He kissed her nose. "Are you ready to get married? It could help with the sleeping arrangements."

She stepped back with a smirk. "Ha! I see where this is going."

He crossed his arms and met her step. "Hey, I am just looking out for everyone."

She shook her head. "I'll marry you, Mr. Chapelle, but sharing a bed, that isn't going to work at this time. We have three guys and four girls, and only three rooms."

A big smile that revealed his beautiful teeth broke out across his face, melting her heart per usual. "Exactly. Eri, Helena, and Alicia in one. Charlie and Myers in the other. And you and me…" He pulled her in by the waist. "Share the third."

It actually made sense. He kissed her softly, sending chills up her spine. "Charlie!" they said in unison.

****

Laura and Bryce stood across from each other, just feet away from the stream in their new back yard. Charlie stood between them with a Bible. The rest of the group sat on the log, smiling and giggling at the fun of this adventure. Even Myers, who they feared would be upset, seemed in good spirits.

"Dearly beloved, we are gathered here for this most wonderful occasion, to unite our awesome friends in Holy Matrimony." He winked at Bryce and smiled at Laura, then opened the Bible. "The scriptures say in Ecclesiastes four, starting in verse nine: 'Two are better than one…' I'm paraphrasing, but if either of you fall down, you are able to help the other up. If either of you need to keep warm, you can do so. If either of you need protection, you have each other's back." He closed the Bible and grabbed both of their hands. "A cord of three strands is not easily broken. Bryce, repeat after me, 'I Bryce.' "

"I, Bryce."

"Take you, Laura, to be my wife."

"Take you, Laura, to be my wife," Bryce echoed.

"To have and to hold, from this day forward, for better, for worse, for richer, for poorer, in sickness and in health, to love and to cherish, until death do us part, unto God."

Bryce smiled and Laura swooned. "To have and to hold, from this day forward, for better, for worse, for richer, for poorer, in sickness and in health, to love and to cherish, until death do us part, unto God."

Charlie turned to Laura and repeated the same vows. "Then by the power vested in me by the holy Church on the glorious Web, and among God and our friends, I now pronounce you husband and wife. You may kiss your bride."

The couple leaned in and kissed. Laura felt electricity transmit into every part of her body. So much joy after so much pain—it was exhilarating.

"I now introduce to everyone, Mom and Pop Chappelle," Charlie joked.

Laura rolled her eyes, and everyone laughed.

"Let's party," Bryce said. "I just got hitched!" He lifted her in one fell swoop, sending butterflies through her stomach. She kissed him as he walked her to the table.

"Wow!" she said, as he dropped her to her feet.

The table had quite the spread.

"We did the best feast we could muster with mostly canned food and dried goods," Charlie said.

Charlie and Eri had laid out canned three-bean salad, fruit cocktail, beef stew, collard greens, and biscuits. For the wedding cake, they made pineapple upside down pancakes, complete with little bride and groom figurines made out of twigs and toilet paper.

"Everything looks really good. I'm starved," Bryce said.

"Dig in," Charlie said.

The food was surprisingly good. The company was better. Laura could not believe she had married this man. Only two years ago, her life had seemed forlorn, robotic, dead. Then he came in and changed everything. Someone from the outside may think all the running and shooting would make life worse than before, but it was hardly the truth. No, she was free. Free to love the man she cared about. Never would she have had this as an agent in S.I.U. Fraternization was forbidden and ended in murder. She would give up the comforts of stability for love any day. *Until death do us part.*

Chapter Fourteen

Myers tried to evade the gnawing feeling in his gut. On one hand, he was happy for his friends. But he also knew he would never have the same. Sadness overwhelmed him. He needed to take a walk. Leaving the cabin, he spotted Helena just before the tree line. Though he would like to be alone, it was his job to follow her. In all reality, the chore had not been arduous. He enjoyed her company. Often she made him laugh, and there was a strong quality about her. Something he appreciated in women. But that was as far as the attraction went. He was not in the market.

Helena spun around. "You want to join me?"

He grinned. "Is it that obvious?"

A smile lit up her face, once again revealing that beautiful dimple. The gold flecks in her brown eyes danced in joy. It lessened the sadness that consumed his own. "I would love your company. I'm on a mission to find some sort of berries or herbs."

"Sounds fun."

"Besides, I have something for you." She ran on ahead.

"You do?" He sprinted after her, through the trees, down a small path, that eventually led to a thin steady stream. "What is it? I am not a big fan of surprises."

She stopped suddenly, and he almost smacked into her. "Don't be absurd. Everyone says that. But they really do love surprises."

He sat on a log a few feet away and shrugged. "Not me. I like to know what's coming."

She stood in front of him and knelt down to his eye level. "I might be able to change your mind."

"Good luck trying." She held out a small paper bag, the one he had seen her grab in the store. "Surprise."

Slowly and unsure, he took the bag.

"Go on, open it." She pushed up and sat on the log next to him.

He looked and then reached inside. It was the knife from the store. He lifted it out, with gratitude, but also disdain. "Why did you buy this for me?"

She shrugged. "You seemed like you needed a pick me up. I heard you lost someone."

His eyes narrowed. "Not someone. My fiancé." Grief cascaded through him, willing him to cry. He pushed it back. "I'm not available."

"You say that now. You're young. Time will heal." She touched his hand.

He recoiled and leapt to his feet. "You can't possibly understand what I'm going through."

Helena jumped up across from him, her eyes on fire. "Oh really! You think you're the only one who has lost someone. The only one to watch someone, who you love dearly, be shot right in front of you? I watched that butcher place a gun to my father's head and pull the trigger. His blood was on my clothes and in my hair for almost a week. I had to bear the smell of his rotting corpse, because I was frightened. I didn't have a group of friends like you have to take me away from it all. I was forced to bear it, because I didn't have the strength to lift him, to bury him on my own." Tears cascaded down her cheeks. "You and I are more alike than you know. I loved my father. I miss him every day. And no one should ever have to experience that. Someday you'll fall in love again. I will never have my father again." Without warning, she hurdled over the log and ran up the bank back toward the cabin.

I am a jerk. Lost in his own anguish, he failed to realize that others were hurting too. Of course, he should have been more compassionate. He stared out at the stream. The water softly babbled over the smooth rock bed, airing a relaxing sound of pitter-patter trickling down toward a small waterfall a few feet away. Chords of light streamed through the trees above, glistening off the fluid train. If only his heart could match the tranquility of this place. If they had chosen a desert, that would have been closer to how he felt. Dry, brittle, dead.

The trees rustled behind him. He stood and faced them with his new knife poised. Helena had returned. A sheepish expression covered her pretty features.

"I'm sorry," she said.

He shook his head. "Nah, it was me. I was being selfish, as always. Assuming I'm the only one in the universe with a broken heart. I think the whole wedding thing just made me a tad cranky."

"May I?" She pointed to the log.

"Please. Let's start again." He held out his hand and smiled. "Hi, I'm Myers. I just turned nineteen, love computer hacking, and enjoy the occasional robbery. Newly reformed, and trying to not insert my mouth where it does not belong."

She giggled. "And I am Helena. Age twenty-three.

Love hand-to-hand combat and painting when I'm not running for my life."

He grinned. "Twenty-three? We all thought you were sixteen. Seventeen at the most."

"Yes, I get that a lot. A diminutive stature and Puerto Rican skin—it preserves me well. I may hate it now, but it will serve me well when I am older."

"I was talking about your maturity level." He winked.

She hit him playfully.

He laughed. "Hand-to-hand, huh? We should spar some each day. Getting in shape will be important for all of us."

"I would like that." She lifted a rock and tossed it into the drink. It plopped with a slight smash and sank to the bottom. "I am sorry for your loss. Death hurts."

"Yeah. Ditto."

They both sighed and stared at the stream, not moving, not caring, lost in their thoughts, well into the rest of the day.

****

The next day, armed with sticks they found in the woods, Helena swung and Myers blocked. She spun around and swung again. He blocked. His arm swung down to her legs and knocked her down. She flipped over and bounced back up.

"Dirty," she said.

"You have to be prepared for anything."

She nodded. "Again."

He aimed the stick for her face. She blocked, then countered. He blocked. Back and forth, the swung, hit, blocked, each one missing. Something moved in the trees. Both in unison swung with weapons ready for battle.

"May I?" Laura smiled

Myers lifted an eyebrow and nodded for Helena to surrender her stick.

"Oh, I know I can beat you. I trained you. I was talking about her." Laura pointed to Helena. "I need to see what she can do."

Myers nodded and handed his stick to Laura. This would be good. He backed to the log and sat.

Laura held the stick with both hands diagonally in front of her. Slowly, she circled Helena. Fear was evident in Helena's face. Laura was the best. If someone could take all of them out, she could. Only Eri came close to Laura's skill set, but even then, Eri hadn't beaten her yet.

Helena swung.

Laura blocked and swung, dropping Helena to her knees. "You have to anticipate what your opponent will do."

The woman got back up and shifted her feet in the dirt, shifting her stick vertical to the sky.

Both charged, and the sticks clanked against each other. Several times, they knocked. Then Helena went high. Laura ducked and struck her in the side.

"Ouch!" Helena stumbled back. "How?"

"Look for tells. The eyes, the body, the way the feet point, the muscles and how they contract—everything tells you something. Learn what I do." Laura pitched the stick forward and Helena blocked. "Better."

Hit. Block. Hit. Block. "Good. Again."

Sweat beaded on Helena's lip. Her hair damp against her temples, with an expression of determination, she lunged forward. Laura ducked, but not quick enough. The stick scraped the side of her face.

"Yes!" Laura smiled and tossed the stick back to Myers. "Keep working, but don't go easy on her. I know you were."

Great, did she have to reveal that?

Not seeming to care about the red mark on her cheek, Laura bowed to Helena as a sign of respect, waved, and disappeared back through the trees.

"That woman amazes me." Myer chuckled.

"So, you were going easy?"

He gave a sheepish smile. "Well, maybe a little."

"Well—" Helena held the stick high, "—don't."

Chapter Fifteen

Eri sat on a bench by the bay window in the cabin, reading a book of poetry she found in a small bookshelf. The forest outside appeared serene, a calm she often did not feel herself. It relaxed her. Her eyes caught a blue jay a few feet away. Its bright electric blue feathers were decorated with a mosaic white and periwinkle design. A pointed cap sat on its head, reminding her of a teacher she once had. She followed it with her eyes, as it hopped from branch to branch. Charlie passed the window, and it fluttered away. Her pulse increased. Never had any man held her heart. This was all new. The feelings she was experiencing were foreign. How did she navigate them? Seeing Laura and Bryce marry made her experience hope in a new way. Though crazy to assume, it was possible for them to have a real life. Someday, somewhere. With him?

"What are you doing in here all alone?" Charlie asked, walking inside and sitting next to her on the cushioned bench.

"Nothing." She turned and stretched. "Just reading. Thinking."

"About me?" He winked.

Maybe. Though she'd never reveal that. Though she was a tough girl, this boy made her soft. "Want to go for a walk? I think when the snow comes, we won't be able to experience days like this much longer."

"You never have to ask."

They waited until they were a few yards away from the cabin, before Charlie laced his fingers with hers. It felt natural, right. As strange as they were as a couple, it was like they had been together forever. Many say opposites attract. Whatever the cosmic reason for that, it aligned with them perfectly. Maybe it was God's way of sending balance to the world. In their case, they made a good team. She just wished they could talk about it.

"Bryce said they really enjoyed the food yesterday," Charlie said. "If I hadn't been such a computer geek, I just may have done the whole culinary thing. I actually enjoy it."

"Making canned food taste good. That is an art." Eri kicked a rock and then smiled. "You're good. Not as good as me. But good."

"Hey!" He playfully pushed her with his arm. "Until you made that Chinese feast, you destroyed our food. Must I bring up the word *tacos*? I think if we had everyone vote about the best cook, they would mark that against you." He winked.

"Hmm, maybe." Eri saw a couple of rocks and sat on one. Her mind returned to her thoughts in the cabin. "Do you think we will ever experience normal? You and I?"

He shrugged and joined her on the adjoining rock. "What is normal for us, really? Maybe this is. This isn't so bad, right?" He pulled her close and kissed her cheek. "I really do not mind as long as you're in my 'normal'."

"It's not *our* normal. It is some snowbird's house and supplies from an elderly person's attic. None of this is ours." Eri sighed. "What is our normal? Stealing other people's lives?"

Charlie kneeled on the ground next to her and touched her chin. "This family isn't normal to most people, but it is good. The love we all have for each other. The things we can do. It's pretty wonderful. We can take care of each other and are not alone in all this." He cupped her hand in his. "We will find our roots someday. I promise. We just have to wait for the perfect timing. That's all."

She leaned toward him. Their lips touched. Her hands threaded through his long blond hair. The warmth of his mouth shocked her senses. Every part of her melted into his caress.

A twig snapped, and they jumped back.

Oh no. Laura stood just feet away. Her expression cold, unrevealing. They were in trouble for sure.

Eri sensed the heat rising in her cheeks. She stood and faced her leader, afraid to speak. More scared not to. Leave it to Charlie to prattle.

"Um, she lost something, and I was trying to—"

Laura held up a hand and grinned.

Why is she smiling?

"I already knew," Laura said. "I saw you kiss in the attic."

Charlie exhaled, standing to his feet, obviously as relieved as Eri was.

"Are you mad?" Eri asked.

"No." Laura shook her head. "How could I be? I just married Bryce." She held up her hand, revealing the ring they had fashioned from twine and rope. "Look, my only concern is to be extremely careful. You have seen firsthand what happens when you get close to someone in this lifestyle." Her eyes flashed down the hill, probably thinking of Myers. "But I've been part of the forbidding love game at S.I.U., and I am not a fan. It is painful and wrong. If you two like each other, then live. Love. Who am I to stop that?" She offered a closed mouth smile.

"Thanks," Eri said, relieved.

"Don't keep it a secret." Laura touched her shoulder. "Be honest with your family. We have too much happening to not be honest. Know what I'm saying?"

Eri and Charlie nodded.

"We'll tell them tonight," Charlie said.

"Good. As you were." Laura laughed and walked back down the hill.

Eri laughed, falling into Charlie's chest. "I can't believe she saw us kissing. So embarrassing."

"But at least she was cool about the whole thing." He brought her chin up and kissed her lightly on the lips. "And she's right. We need to stop hiding it. For one, because I really like you and would like to stop pretending I don't. And second, no secrets. We've had enough of that."

Eri chewed the side of her cheek and offered a coy smile. "Yeah, okay. But I'll do it, all right?"

Charlie looked at her sideways. "You don't trust me?"

She gave a side grin with a raised eyebrow. "Would you?"

"Probably not."

She kissed his lips, soft, tender, and then looked him in the eye. "I'm glad you found me."

"Found you?"

"People are lost. But your heart, it found mine. I'm glad."

He tucked a strand of a hair behind her ear and kissed her cheek. He pulled back and stared in her eyes. If they weren't careful, they would fall hard. Maybe they had already. He kissed her again. "Ready to go inside?"

She smiled. "Probably should. The sun is setting, and it's getting cold."

He lifted her to her feet and wrapped his arm around her shoulders. "And for the record, I'm glad you found me, too."

****

The group sat around the room playing charades. Eri had never really liked an activity that made her act silly for the sake of people watching. But without many options for entertainment, they were forced to do what they could. Myers promised to find them a deck of cards the next time they went to town.

Eri glanced at Charlie, who stared at her with that "come on" look. *Fine. Time to get it out of the way.* "Hey, everyone, I have an announcement."

All eyes focused on her. Her mouth felt dry. She licked her lips. "Charlie and I are together." She lowered her head and quickly sat back down.

Silence. Then laughter.

"We already knew," Myers said.

"What?" Eri said lifting her head.

"It would have been more fun if you had made that into a charade," Charlie said, cupping his hand in hers. "But thanks for breaking the ice."

"How did you know?" Eri asked.

"We all saw you kissing in the attic," Helena said.

"All of you?" Eri felt horrified as they all nodded.

Myers must have sensed her embarrassment. He jumped up, rubbing his hand together and said, "Okay, my turn." He held out a fist and turned the other in a circular motion.

"Movie," Charlie said.

Myers nodded, cupped his hands in front of him, and then pushed them forward.

"Boat!" Helen yelled.

He hit his nose, then made a fist with his left hand, and brought his right hand, still cupped, into the side of the fist.

"Titanic," Laura said.

"Yes!" Myers laughed. "One point for you again. I think we can safety say Laura wins hands down."

"It may be time for a new activity," Eri said, hoping she didn't have to take a turn.

"Yeah, probably." Myers flopped back on the couch. "I don't get how someone who was deprived of most of her adolescence and early adulthood is so in touch with pop culture."

Laura pushed her legs up to her chest and wrapped her hands around them. "That's because at S.I.U. we were trained in pop culture. There were times we had to infiltrate regular people. I even did two short term assignments in a public high school."

Helena and Alicia got up to get something from the kitchen.

"And you didn't try to escape?" Charlie asked.

The same thought had occurred to Eri. Their team couldn't wait long enough to have one assignment to leave. Why didn't Laura leave when she was free?

The sisters entered with coffee, whispering.

"No, by that time, I was completely indoctrinated." Laura sighed. "I had no desire to run. I was part of the system, and they knew that. Besides, they were always watching. I was not sent in alone. We were assured a sniper was always trained on the situation. If I didn't perform, the target would get a bullet. Then I would. There was no freedom. Not even in the field." She ran a hand through her black hair, obviously thinking. "My partner…"

Eri flashed back to Laura's partner, Harding. The man betrayed them, and then helped them. None of that ever made much sense to her.

Laura eyes clouded.

"What's wrong?" Bryce asked.

Laura stood and faced the room. "I think I know who shot Julio."

Helena and Alicia stopped talking and stared at her, eyes wide, scared.

Bryce stood next to her and grabbed her hand. "Who?

"Harding," she said.

Chapter Sixteen

Laura exhaled. At her mention of her partner, she knew. Harding was the one running things now. He was the head that sprung up to take Greenstone's place. While her former boss was incarcerated, it was Harding that would hunt them. Or would he? He had helped them once before. Might he leave them alone now? No, she understood the way he thought. The plan to kill Julio and kidnap Alicia had all been in some grand scheme of capturing Laura again. But why? She rubbed her temples. Pain shot through her head. She needed sleep to ward off the migraine, but it was obvious none would come tonight.

Bryce wrapped his hand around her waist. "What's going on in your mind?"

"I don't know why I know, but I just figured out Harding is to blame for all of this. He is extremely good at tracking. He will find us. We have got to sort out a plan now and move on."

He led her to one of the couches and sat with her. The group folded around her to face the conversation. "We still have a few months. No one knows we're here."

"What about the postcard?" Helena asked.

Laura united her stare. "We never mailed it. It was just a ploy."

Instantly, Alicia's body language changed. Her

head bowed, and her hands began to fidget with an afghan hanging from the couch. Years of training allowed Laura to see the body language of everyone in the room. Her heart sank. She sat forward on the couch. "Alicia, what did you do?"

"You weren't using it, and it had a stamp."

"Alicia, what did you do?" Laura asked again, heat rising up her skull and into her eyes.

"I mailed it to our Aunt Rosa in Ponce," Alicia said. "I didn't want her to worry, in case she went to see Papá."

Everyone started yelling, mumbling angry retorts her way.

Myers, of course, started cursing and pacing. Charlie began grabbing things and stuffing them in the bags they'd brought. Bryce bowed his head, scratching the sides of his temples. Eri stood perfectly still, almost statue-like, glaring at Alicia. That frightened Laura the most. Eri was capable of a lot damage without notice. Laura glanced at Bryce. He looked to her. The panic in his eyes matched the alarm in her soul. This was not good. Not at all. How long did they have?

"Why did you do that, you stupid litt—" Myers stepped toward her.

Helena blocked him. "Don't you dare touch her!"

"Do you have any idea what she has done?" He paced like a caged animal, face red, fists clenching. "This move is on her." He kicked a chair and then punched a wall. Nothing could console him.

Laura knew that. There was a part of her that would love to throw a tantrum as well. She squeezed her eyes shut, not sure what to do next.

"Why is this such a big deal?" Helena asked.

"You're all acting crazy."

Myers spun back to her and walked within an inch of her face. "It's a big deal, because Alicia just gave away the one thing we had going for us—amenity. No one knew where we were. Now they do."

"I didn't write the return address." Alicia's voice cracked with an ounce of hope. "How could they?"

"So stupid!" Myers walked away and began pacing again. "Idiotic!"

"Calm down, Myers," Bryce said, walking toward him. "This isn't helping. We need to figure something out."

Myers threw his hands out and folded to the ground like an angry child.

Charlie tossed a full bag at the door and faced Alicia. "Ever heard of a postmark? It puts the bad guys in our backyard. These aren't just run of the mill fans. These are people who are trained to seek and destroy. If they want to find us, they will. You just gave them the biggest heads up. Thanks!"

"But how?" Tears welled in Alicia's eyes. "I don't get it."

"All they have to do is stop by that Outpost, ask a few questions of that old guy, and they'd have us in minutes." Charlie walked to another bag and started stuffing more blankets and supplies.

"No, I meant from my aunt's mailbox?"

"Trust me. If she is connected to you, they were checking her mail." Charlie zipped that bag closed and tossed it by the other one.

Eri stated almost trance-like. "We never should have brought them with us."

"We have to go now," Laura said and then looked

at her new husband. "The honeymoon is over."

He kissed her cheek and then walked to the kitchen.

With the exception of Alicia, who was too distraught, everyone else started stuffing things in bags, boxes, and trunks. Laura had a tad bit of compassion for the girl, but it was quickly fading. How did she get a letter out without them noticing? Laura had to also blame herself. A warning about the telephone was given to Myers, not thinking about the postcard was stupid. Also, not explaining the whys and hows to Alicia was also on her. How could they expect this girl to understand their world?

"Fifteen minutes, we're gone," Laura said, then started up the stairs.

Her team worked fast. They had spent the last year doing this very thing. Packing and running. It was what they did and who they were. For better or for worse, they were always the lost few floating from place to place with no real future and no real home.

****

A flicker of light caught Laura's eye, the small flash danced in the distance.

"Everybody down," she yelled, slamming the front door with her foot. Everyone dropped in obedience, eyes wide. "Where are the guns?"

Charlie frowned. "In the van."

"We need them now!" She cycled through options. *No one's dying this time.*

"I'll go." Eri crouched toward the stairs.

Charlie grabbed her arm. "Don't be dumb."

"I'm not."

"You're not going."

Determination tethered her eyes. "Yes, I am. I'm the stealthy one, the fastest—I'm your ninja, remember? I'm going."

Laura nodded. "Okay, we have to create a distraction. Eri, go." She glanced at Myers who descended from the stairs. "Are the lights off up there?"

He flashed an 'ok' sign.

"Could you see anything?"

"There's a black van to the west, but I didn't spot any shooters."

"I did." Laura motioned with her head for Eri to go.

Eri darted up the stairs.

Charlie breathed shallowly; eyes fixed where Eri had gone. People in this business don't fall in love. It takes their focus, and it makes them weak.

A black canister smashed through a window and bounded against the carpet. With a pop, CS gas seeped from the grenade.

Laura hustled everyone into the small kitchen, then slammed the door closed. A film of smoke blotted her vision. Pain burnt her lungs as she began wheezing, along with the others in the room, coughing, gasping. "Find something to cover your mouths," Laura gasped. Her eyes burned with an acidic irritation that spread across the rest of her skin and into her lungs. Each breath burdened a sharp constriction. Snot ran from her nose to the floor. Oxygen eluded her. She slipped a rag from a drawer to cover the crack at the bottom of the door. Charlie passed out dishtowels. Laura grabbed one and tied it around her face. She wrestled to swallow a deep breath.

A loud thud echoed outside the door. Eri must have

dropped in from the balcony with duffle bag that held their weapons. She cracked open the door.

"You amaze me," Charlie said. "I can't even imagine how you pulled it off, but it must have been sweet."

"What did you see?" Laura asked through haggard breaths.

"We cannot exit from the front." Eri pointed toward the door. "There are men there."

"I'm surprised they haven't fired yet. That worries me." Bryce's reflection peered back from a mirror he held toward the window. "Ideas, Agent Black?"

"That would be Agent Chappelle to you, sir. Drop the mirror, they'll see you." She peered around the space.

"There can't be two of us," he said, hiding the mirror.

"Good point. Hyphenated name it is." She winked. "Totally open to ideas."

"There is a hole behind the dryer. Don't suppose we could..." Helena said.

Laura crab-walked to the small room just off the kitchen. They had a laundry room, but their bathroom was outside. Weird. Bryce and she moved the dryer to the side. A gaping hole lay behind it. Big enough for Eri, not big enough for Myers.

"Now what?" Myers asked.

"If we break it, it might make noise," Laura said.

"We could be a distraction up front while you dig." Myers thrust a bullet into his chamber and nodded to the living room.

"Okay, Myers, you and I will go. The rest of you work on this hole and signal us when it is done." Laura tied the red cotton dishtowel around her face and exited the space. Laura glanced out the window. One man crossed her path. She fired through the pane. The guy dropped.

Bullets cackled behind her head. The wooden mantel ruptured. Myers fired back. An exchange of more rounds whizzed above Laura's head. A whistle came from the doorway. Bryce motioned for her to follow.

Laura made herself small as she slid to the kitchen. Myers slunk behind her.

The gunfire stopped, followed by the clicking of boots outside the front door.

They closed the door and Myers, Charlie, and Bryce overturned the kitchen table to form a barricade against the doorway. All color drained from Alicia's face.

"Alicia," snapped Laura. "Are you still with us?"

The girl gave a slight nod.

The table exploded with the firing of machine guns and rifles.

"Stay low," Laura barked.

"We have to go," Bryce roared.

Laura turned to Eri. "Take us out."

"Follow my footsteps exactly." She shot Helena and Alicia a stern expression. "Do not make a sound."

They stared with a blank expression back at Eri.

Eri slinked out the hole like a cat. The group fumbled out the wall after her. They crawled out to a range of bushes that gave them limited cover. The biggest of the bunch, Myers scraped his arm attempting to squeeze through. His face grimaced, but he managed to not scream.

Helena stopped and looked back.

"Come on." Myers held out a hand to her.

"Alicia!" Helena screamed back toward the room.

Adrenaline fired through Laura's veins, the girl wasn't with them. "Eri, you may have to—"

A man walked around the corner, and all guns snapped to his position. He held Alicia in his arms with a pistol to her head. "Put down your weapons, or I'll shoot—"

A gun fired, and the man crumpled to the ground. All eyes shifted to Myers and his smoking gun.

"He was wide open." He shrugged.

Dismissing the risk, they group dashed for the van. An eruption of gunfire followed them from the house, across the trees, and against the dirt. They piled in. Myers revved the engine. "Do we deal with them or run?"

"We made it out." Laura cocked her weapon. "We run."

Chapter Seventeen

Eri leaned her head against Charlie's shoulder and cried. His hand caressed her hair, as he tried to console her. Over the past few years, she had become tough, but she was tired, overwhelmed. So tired of running. Sad to see so much pain. For only a moment, they had experienced paradise. As always, it was fleeting. Gone before it set in.

"We haven't lost them, folks." Myers stared in the review mirror, as he gunned the engine. "Get your guns locked and loaded."

Eri popped up to peek out the back window, when a bullet shot the glass just missing the left side of her head.

Myers swerved and then punched the gas again. The van shot forward. "Anyone hurt?"

The group echoed, "No."

"Everybody, stay low to floor." Laura opened the pantry on the kitchenette and pulled out some foil and duct tape. She tossed it to Charlie. "You and Eri secure the windows."

Charlie nodded.

Eri hoped this worked. She took the box end, and Charlie ripped off some of the tape. The two of them pulled it across before getting on the bench. They both tried to stay to the walls as they adhered it. Within seconds, bullets pelted the windows and back, holes now visible through the foil.

Alicia screamed.

Glass shattered down, but not out due to the foil. It had helped in that short time.

The group all pushed their bodies into the carpet, close to the walls. Bryce left the passenger seat and crouched behind the small refrigerator. "I'm open to suggestions."

"Myers, let me drive," Eri said. "You guys are better at shooting."

She climbed in front of him into the seat as he climbed out behind her. It was a bit awkward, but they did it without too much deviating. Helena and Alicia bunched up by the passenger seat, looking extremely uncomfortable. The clicks of guns and rifles could be heard in the back.

Eri floored it. The road was a tad icy, causing her to swerve a bit, but she handled it. The good news was the road was desolate. Except for the occasional bend, it was easy to navigate. In the side mirror, she could see the SUV starting to cross into the other lane and make their way around to the front. "They're going to be even with me soon if you do not do something."

Several of them started firing out the back van widow.

The SUV floored it, coming up on the driver's side.

"Gun!" Charlie leaned over her and fired out the driver's window.

She tried to stay straight, but it was hard with him there.

Laura pulled the foil down.

The SUV swerved and dropped back. As soon as it was behind the van again, the team fired. Ear shattering cracks and the smell of sulfur and gun oil, and the haze of smoke filled the cabin. Eri glanced in the rearview mirror.

Only Laura had her gun up. She fired. A hole pierced where the driver sat. The SUV swerved and veered off the side of the small incline.

Eri shouted, "Yes."

Myers crossed to the front to take the reins of driving again. Eri slid out.

"Did you get them?" Helena said from behind the passenger's seat.

"Yes." Laura grabbed a towel from one of the bags and wiped the bench free of glass and sat. "But I'm sure they have already informed people where we are. We need to disappear now. Myers, the first chance you can get off this—"

He swerved, hitting a dirt path that looked more like a hiking trail than a road. Trees scraped the sides, and the van bounced like a bucking bronco.

"I'm glad we're on the same page." Laura laughed. "Status report."

"We're okay," Helena said.

"Good," Eri said, curling up against the van door, relieved.

"Ditto," Charlie said, sitting next to her.

Bryce crawled next to Laura and pointed to small cut on her forehead. "We're good, but looks like you have some glass in your head."

She touched it and winced.

"Here, lean back." She placed her head against the cushion back, and Bryce leaned over her with a knife. "Sorry for this."

A scraping sound resonated, and then Laura

screamed. The bumpy road didn't help. It was over fast, but by Laura's response, it didn't feel good. Blood seeped down her face like tears. Bryce used the edge of his shirt to wipe it from her face.

Eri reached into one of the bags and handed him a washcloth from the cabin. "Here."

"Thanks." He poured some water on it from a bottle and held it to Laura's head.

"Now that our windows are gone, it's crazy cold in here." Eri sat back and rested her head on the van door.

Charlie wrapped his arm around her and brought her closer.

"Where is the bag with blankets?" Helena said.

Eri pointed by Bryce's foot.

Helena climbed over Charlie and Eri's feet and knelt at the box. She pulled a brown wool one out and handed it to Bryce, who placed it over Laura. Then she pulled out a blue sleeping bag and handed it to Charlie. He unzipped it and flapped it open, to lay over both of him and Eri.

Eri leaned her head against his shoulder.

Charlie intertwined his fingers with hers.

Despite all cold and the movement of the van, Eri managed to fall asleep.

****

The van came to a sudden stop. Eri opened her eyes. Charlie was no longer with her but in the driver's seat. Myers was a few inches away, asleep at her feet. "Why are we stopping?"

Charlie glanced back. "I think we can hang out here for the rest of the day. Leave tonight."

Eri turned and opened the side door. Everyone poured out. Where were they? A warm, dry wind caressed her face. The landscape was barren and parched. With the exception of a few semi-trucks whizzing by on the interstate, cacti and tumbleweeds were all she could see for miles.

"Well, this is different." She walked around the van and saw they were at rest stop. There were a few picnic tables, bathrooms, and vending machines. *Perfect.*

Eri pulled some clothes, toothpaste, a towel, and soap from one of the bags and started for the restroom. Helena and Alicia joined her. Inside, there were three metal stalls, a sink, but no mirror. She did her best to wash up in the sink and get dressed into a pair of black yoga pants and charcoal gray T-shirt. It, at least, made her feel a bit more human.

Eri glanced around at the team to see what they had all changed into. Helena had slipped on a forest green tank top and jeans. Alicia had on a blue summer dress. After days in the cold, it felt good to be in the heat. Even Charlie, who always wore a hoodie, was just wearing a T-shirt and jeans. Laura, Myers, and Bryce were predictable. They almost always had on the same clothes—black T-shirts with matching cargo pants.

"You looked refreshed," Charlie said.

"I feel a million times better." Eri surveyed the van. Bullet holes decorated the van on all sides. The windows were blown out the back.

"So much for Agent Apparatus," Charlie said. "It's going to be hard to blend in with this."

Laura stepped next to him and nodded. "Yeah, I think we're going to have go shopping again. Myers and Charlie—you know what to do. We can hang out here and rest, and then, we'll leave in something new tonight."

Bryce returned with junk food from the vending machine and tossed it out onto the picnic table. Everyone grabbed a bag.

Eri got cheese fish crackers. *Breakfast of champions*.

The team assembled on the benches to talk strategy for their next move. Helena and Alicia stayed back to rest. The group didn't seem to have any consensus on their next move. Where did they go? The possibilities were endless and not existent. Every time one was suggested, it was tossed out for some reason or another.

"Look…" Myers leapt up from the table and started pacing. "Maybe we stop running and fight."

"We aren't ready—" Laura started to say.

"Ready?" Myers eyes flamed. "They don't care. One way or another, they are coming after us. Either we can be on the defensive, or we can be on the offensive. We can't cower and run any longer. We're wearing down."

Eri popped a cracker in her mouth, considering that. "I think he's right."

Laura's gaze met Eri's. Her expression unclear. Was she mad at her for agreeing or was she contemplating the source? Laura then looked at Bryce. His gaze dropped to his hands for a second, and then he said, "I think we should fight."

All eyes fell to Charlie. He nodded. "Yeah, fight."

Myers punched his fist. "Yes!"

"Okay then, we fight." Laura took a visible deep breath and then exhaled through her mouth. "But we need a plan. A good plan."

How did they fight a ghost? "First, we have to

know who we are fighting."

Charlie held up the thumb drive. "We still have this."

"Of course." Laura grinned. "With everything, I completely forgot we had that. Charlie, plug it in. We have a war to wage."

Chapter Eighteen

Myers suddenly felt alive again. Though he often pretended to be coping well with everything, he was far from okay. His emotions were on some sort of elevator ride. One minute he was angry, the next sad, but never happy, that emotion alluded him. Though he would never admit it out loud, Helena had become a great distraction. Once he realized she understood him, it made it easier to share. No way could he have made it without her friendship. He glanced at her across the table.

She smiled. This fight was for both of them—for her father and his girlfriend. Forget justice, he was out for vengeance. Not just for Denise, but for all of them. They deserved better. They deserved happiness.

Charlie fired up the computer. "It has an encryption code. Give me a second."

Great! Everything in Myers wanted to push Charlie out of the way and do it himself. Truthfully, Charlie was probably the better hacker, though Myers would never admit that. But waiting was painful. Myers paced behind him, willing him to do it. Wanting to take control. With each click of the mouse, Myers cringed. This waiting was not helping keep him calm. He started to walk away.

Charlie clapped. "I'm in."

Myers turned back. Both he and Laura leaned in.

Charlie cracked his knuckles and started clicking the mouse on different files.

"The red one in the lower left corner," Laura said, pointing to the screen.

Charlie clicked on it. *Password protected.* He groaned.

"Man!" Myers turned around and tried to compose himself. This was overwhelming, his heart sat in his gut. So much adrenaline coursed through his veins. Why did he have such emotions? He didn't get this upset before. He squeezed his eyes shut, willing himself not to hit anything.

"I can do this, Myers. Just hang on. No sweat." Charlie clicked out of the thumb drive into some program he had probably installed for such a task. A bar ran across the screen, indicating it was opening.

Myers secretly prayed. No way could he handle this disappointment. His palms were sweaty, his heart raced, and anxiety pulsed through his core. Helena walked next to him and placed a hand on his back. He was too riled up to stand still, but he didn't want to flinch her off. He tried to focus on her hand. Somehow that calmed him.

"It's open," Charlie said.

Myers flipped back around and leaned over again.

Laura touched Charlie's shoulder. "What do we have?"

"A bunch of top-secret documents, budgets, financed operations, and personnel lists." Charlie glanced at both of them. "So much, where do we start?"

"We can stay here at the rest stop for the night and take shifts combing through all of this content." Laura stepped back and looked at each of them. "If anyone finds anything, wake us all up. It'll be a long night, but hopefully by morning, we'll know something."

Myers was encouraged by her petition to find something. Too often she had swept his desires to the back of their agenda. This time, he was at the forefront. He needed that. Anything less and he'd probably go nuts.

"I can take the first shift," Charlie said.

"I call second." Myers slapped him on the back.

"I'll take third," Eri said.

"Fourth," Laura said. "And if we still don't have anything, I'll wake up Bryce. Night everyone."

Everyone said their good nights and climbed in the van. It was a tight squeeze. The team did the best they could to fit around the space with the vain purpose of sleeping. Bryce leaned the driver's seat back as far as it would go, and Laura slept next to him in the passenger's seat, which reclined a bit farther. Helena and Alicia took the bench in back, laying against each other. Eri reclined on the floor in front of the bench and Myers laid down the middle of the van on the shag carpet. The soft rhythm of breath filled the cabin. Myers didn't really plan to sleep. There was no way he would sleep until he had his turn at the computer, and chances are he would let them all sleep until he found something.

They had left the van door open so Charlie could easily grab them if something popped up. Myers reclined on his side, so he could stare at the screen a few feet away. The glow was like a beacon in the dark truck stop filled with only a few semis and the occasional family stopping to use the restroom. Myers couldn't really see any details, but being part of the search made him relax somehow. It was hours before Charlie finally came to wake him.

"Did you sleep at all?" he asked.

Myers laughed. "Hardly. You find anything?"

"Hardly." Charlie smirked.

The two switched places. Like a kid on Christmas, Myers sat at the keyboard, ready to get started. He clicked the first file open. Nothing. He quickly closed it. With each one, he hoped for some great outcome. Nada. He did this for hours. His eyes burned, and his head grew fuzzy. It became time to wake Eri, but he didn't. As frustrated as he was, he wasn't willing to give up for the sense of rest. He knew he wouldn't sleep anyway, so it made more sense to keep going. Click. Close. Click. Close. His head pounded. He shook it off. Click. Close. Click. *Wait.*

What was this? He scanned the page. His heart leapt. Could this be it? "Hey!" Myers jumped up and banged on the van. "Wake up."

Laura was the first up. Charlie was second, followed by the rest rubbing their eyes.

"What did you find?" Laura peered over his shoulder and smiled. "You did it, Myers. We got them."

Chapter Nineteen

Laura and Bryce lay down on a blanket on top of the table and stared up at the stars. As far as honeymoons go, this had to be the strangest. Within five minutes, a soft snore sounded from his mouth. How did he sleep through all this and on a hard table? Her mind was reeling. She had studied the file in detail. Harding was now in charge, which was frightening. He knew her better than anyone else? The perfect enemy. They trained together. Grew up together. Her strike would be his counter.

The other thing that surprised her was Greenstone's kidnapping of her hadn't even been sanctioned. The documents had discussed his permanent dismissal—that was a polite way of saying murder. But it was no wonder. The man had exposed their organization to the world. The biggest thing Laura couldn't digest was his role in all of this. All this time, she believed Greenstone *was* S.I.U. That was apparently not true. Greenstone had been only an arm of the octopus—arms that reached far and wide into many countries. They were not just kidnapping orphans in America anymore. The company was in India, Africa, Europe, and South East Asia.

The best news, however, was S.I.U.'s main location was listed within the files. Well, hopefully. She had to consider the worst. That once they broke into the shell company, S.I.U. moved. Time was not on her team's side. Not that it ever was. They would need to get there quickly. At least it was stateside, but not in great territory. Someone once said the best place to hide is in plain sight. And that is what they had done. S.I.U. now rested in Washington D.C., likely posing as agents. With the enemy so close, it astounded her the feds hadn't busted them. But Laura knew how good S.I.U. was. She had helped with many of those cover-ups. They were very thorough—brilliant even.

A soft desert wind caressed her arms. She pulled a wool blanket from her torso to cover her arms just as a shooting star shot across the sky.

"What did you wish for?" Eri said walking to her side.

"If I tell you, it won't come true, right?"

"I'm sure it is what we all wish for. No secret there." Eri sat on the corner of the bench. "I'm tired of running. We all are."

"I know." Laura sat up and slid to the bench next to her. "I feel the guilt of that every day."

"You? Why?"

"Because I brought you all in." How she wished she could erase the day she went to each of their homes and took them. It sent guilt into her soul.

"But if you hadn't, you'd still be fighting, killing, for them."

"True. But you'd be free." Laura half-smiled.

"Did you come up with our names?"

Laura shook her head. "No. Greenstone did."

Eri touched her shoulder. "If it wasn't you, it would have been someone else, and we would all be dead or in the field. Only you made it change. Only you gave us freedom."

"This is not freedom." Tears welled in Laura's eyes.

"This is not captivity. We still run or don't run. We still hide or fight. It is our call how our ending occurs." She squeezed and pulled her hand back.

Those thoughts had not occurred to her. If anyone else had been assigned to them, the outcome would not have been the same. Never truer words spoken. It gave her a sense of relief that she had not felt in so long. "Thank you."

"For what?"

"You just gave me a gift."

Eri dipped her head. "Then you're very welcome."

Soft orange waves lifted on the horizon awaking the darkened blue sky. Morning. She still had not slept. No worry, they had a long trip ahead of them. She would hopefully relax in the van.

"How are things with you and Charlie?"

Eri lowered her head, something she did when she was embarrassed. Red cheeks were probably part of the deal, but Laura couldn't see them in the violet hue lighting. "They're good, but complicated."

"Complicated, huh? All love is complicated."

Her gaze met Laura's. "How do we really fall in love when we are running for our lives? You, yourself warned against distractions. And he's already shown he may not be able to handle it."

A soft emotion of understanding rolled over Laura, but she couldn't let Eri be discouraged. "Maybe you'll be like Bryce and me and learn to work together. Yes, it can be a distraction, but our bond is strong. I wouldn't go into the field without him again."

She nodded.

Bryce let out a loud snort, and both ladies laughed.

"We should probably wake him and the rest of the group. We have a three day drive ahead of us," Laura said.

"I'll get the van." Eri stood and walked away.

Laura turned her attention to her husband. She leaned over the table and touched her lips to his. Slowly, he woke and kissed her back. "Good morning."

"Good morning to you," he rasped. "Did I sleep long?"

"I gave you about thirty minutes."

"Wow, that long?" He sat up and stretched.

"Well, I wouldn't want you to be groggy." She giggled.

He tilted her chin up and kissed her again. "I assume we are off to D.C. then?"

"Within the hour. We just need to figure out what to eat."

Bryce dropped the ground and sighed. "The closest thing to breakfast we have is canned brown bread and Spam."

"Yum." She laughed and entrenched her arm with his. "Do you ever blame me for bringing you into this life?"

He stepped back. "Why would you ask that?"

She shrugged. "Just wondering."

He took both her hands and pulled her to him. "No. Not for one second. I credit you for getting me out of it."

"That's what Eri said."

Bryce kissed her forehead, her nose, and then her lips. "Because it's true."

"Hey, lovebirds," Charlie said, holding canned bread and Spam up in the air. "Breakfast?"

"Yeah, sounds good," Bryce said, and they both laughed.

****

"Just clean that out and toss…" Laura froze. A black car approached. She reached in the back of her pants and cocked her gun.

Bryce must have noticed, because he stopped pulling boxes from the van, and faced the same direction with the same posture.

It was a limousine. That was a bit odd for a rest stop. Laura readied herself, stepping around the door. They were down two men. Could Bryce, Eri, and her handle this?

Suddenly, Charlie popped up through the hatch in the top of the car. "Surprise!"

Laura laughed. "Charlie, a limo, really?"

"Hey, you said wheels that can hold lots of people. And it's D.C., baby. We'll fit right in."

Myers stepped from the driver's side. "Fresh, right?"

Alicia appeared from the restroom and squealed. "Are we riding in that?"

"We're going to D.C. in style," Charlie said, hopping through the opening and sliding down the car.

Eri greeted him at the ground and kissed his cheek. "You're crazy, you know that?"

"That's what the psychologists tell me." He winked. "You're just jealous because the voices only talk to me."

Eri slapped his arm.

"Do I want to know how you got it?" Laura asked.

"Probably not, but we've disabled any tracker and changed the plates. We're good." Myers grinned. "Let's load up."

Everyone busied themselves with moving boxes from the van to the trunk of the car. Once they were packed, they leapt in. Laura stared at the van. She sure hoped they didn't leave anything damming behind. She had told Alicia to wipe everything down and Helena to look for all forms of hair or other DNA. Hopefully, the girls did a good job.

Bryce walked up behind her. "You okay?"

"Yeah, I'm just worried we've left something behind."

"The girls wiped it of fingerprints, and we checked every crack. We should be good." He pushed a strand from her face. "Which is more than I can say of the cabin. If they're going to incriminate us, it will be there. Can you imagine that poor couple coming home to bullet holes and smashed glass?"

"We need to find SIU so we can get their money and pay for it. All of it. The cars, the clothes, the guns, all of it. I want all these victims taken care of." Laura didn't like adding to her guilt. Everything they did seemed to move them farther from a normal life. She had become the criminal she had run from so many years ago. Whatever she could do to change that, she would. Starting with doing the right thing once this was over.

"That's the best idea yet. Now, let's hit the road, Mrs. Chappell." Bryce touched the small of her back and maneuvered her forward.

"I thought you said there could only be one." She faced back with a sarcastic grin.

"I said there could only be one Agent Chappell, but there is also only one Mrs. Chappell, and that, my dear, is you." He squeezed her shoulders and opened the door for her to climb in.

She shook her head and smiled. For better or worse, she was happy.

Chapter Twenty

Myers sat against the side of the limo, laughing. His stomach hurt from not having used that muscle for so long. Helena made another face, mimicking Laura. The girl could act. Myers glanced up to Laura who was driving. Hopefully, she wasn't hurt. It looked like she was not really paying attention. *Good.*

"You would have made a good agent," Myers said. "I had a hard time with the acting part."

"Acting part?"

"Yeah, part of our training. Acting classes."

Eri frowned. "I hate anything that puts me in front of people. I preferred the martial arts training."

Charlie clapped his hands. "You all are weak. Acting was my favorite part."

Myers laughed. "That's because you have mad scamming skills."

Bryce spun around in the passenger seat and smiled. "We all know who is the best actor out of all of us."

The team said in unison. "Laura."

Myers thought of Denise for a second. She would have been voted at least second. He shook it off.

"What?" Laura said, now obviously tuning back in.

Charlie lowered his voice real deep. "And the best actress award goes to...Laura Black."

"Chappell," Bryce corrected.

"Laura Chappell…" Myers said.

Laura laughed. "Hey, I had acting classes every Tuesday for my entire adolescence. If I am not good, then that would just be sad."

"I still don't get why you need acting classes," Helena asked, sliding from a cushion to the floor of the limo.

"Most of the jobs require us to go undercover as someone other than ourselves." Myers stretched out next to her. "Being able to act can really benefit the case. If the mark does not believe you are who you say you are, that is a huge problem. It could get you killed."

"This agent thing sounds like fun. Acting, martial arts, shooting guns—I wouldn't want to get out. Were you crazy?" She laughed.

Such an innocent thing to say, but the merriment halted, and the space grew tense. No one said anything as heads drooped. Slowly, Myers turned to face Helena. Her eyes appeared sad, her mouth turned down. Clearly, she didn't understand what she had said, or what she was in for. In short, he felt sorry for her.

"We left, because we didn't want to kill innocent people anymore," Laura answered firmly.

"But you still kill," Alicia said, adding gas to the flame. "I saw you shoot those two men in the alley and at the cabin—"

By the way Laura gripped the steering wheel, it was probably good she was driving. Myers considered closing the window between them.

Eri glared at her. Her mouth opened, as if to speak, then snapped closed, probably holding her tongue. Instead, she stared out the window.

What did he say? Yes, they had murdered men a

few days ago. But the argument was in the words.

As if Bryce read his mind, he spoke up. His tone was stern and cross. "She said *innocent* people. Those men were not innocent. If we didn't kill them, they would have killed us. Self-defense is not the same thing. S.I.U. makes children younger than Alicia, hold a gun, and pull the trigger. We were not willing to do that for any man."

The tension mounted like a wall of snow.

"Look, we're sorry." Helena sat back on the bench. "Clearly, we are in a world we don't understand."

"Then you shouldn't have come," Eri said.

"Eri!" Myers knew Eri felt that way, but he hardly expected her to keep voicing it.

"What? I'm sorry, but it is true. I keep saying it, and no one listens. These two girls are untrained and ignorant. They are a liability."

A tear cascaded down Alicia's face.

The fire in Helena's eyes appeared more upset than sad. "If we had stayed, we would have been killed. You have insinuated that a few times, Eri, and the truth is, I would rather take my chances running with the likes of you, then waiting to die at home alone."

"The *likes of us*?" Eri stood the best she could in the limo, eyes narrowed, probably to rip the girl's head off. "What do you know about the likes of us?"

Myers scooted between them. "Okay, put the claws away, ladies. This isn't helping."

Bryce leaned over and whispered to Laura. She nodded and signaled to get over. Good idea. They had been cooped up in the car too long. Fresh air was obviously something they desperately needed.

Eri sat down in a humph and stared out the window

again.

Myers faced Helena. "You just stepped on a land mind. We've lost people, and this journey has been really hard. We've been on the run for over a year. It's like any time you bring someone new on a team; they haven't gone through same experiences. There is no way you can fully understand."

She lowered her head and nodded. "Entiendo."

He needed to change the topic. Maybe he could kill two birds with one stone. Get her some credibility. Eri needed to see the girls' value or this would never end. "So, you said you learned to shoot?"

Her head lifted, and she offered a small smile. "Yeah, I used to hunt with my dad every spring."

"Were you any good?" He smiled and gave a side-glance at Eri.

Her ear was out; she was listening.

"Yeah, I shot my first monkey when I was only seven."

Charlie glanced at her with one raised eyebrow. "You shoot monkeys? How sad."

She laughed. "Yes, we actually have to. They are known to over populate and threaten agriculture of the area. Not to mention, they are quite the nuisance. The government would sometimes pay my father to kill them."

"Do you eat them?" Myers asked.

"Sure." She shrugged. "We always eat what we kill." She pointed at Alicia. "Alicia is great at wrangling snakes. She has killed twelve."

Eri peeked over on that.

"Snakes, really?" Charlie asked.

Alicia sat up and smiled. "Yeah, the best time to

get them is when they are asleep. I knock them out of the tree and hit their head before they are fully aware of what is happening to them."

"And snake tastes good," Helena said.

"I hear it tastes like chicken," Charlie muttered.

Alicia and Helena exchanged an amused smile. "Actually, when fried, it tastes more like a tilapia fish."

Charlie laughed. "Who knew?"

The limo stopped and Laura said through the crack. "Everyone out. We need a serious restroom and food break."

Eri popped the door and hurried off.

The rest of the group took their time climbing out. They were located at what looked like a trucker's greasy spoon. Maybe they'd have some fried chicken. All that talk about chicken made Myer's mouth water for some.

"Are we eating here?" Myers asked.

Laura nodded. "We might as well."

The group strolled toward the entrance. Myers hung back with Helena. For some reason, he had developed a soft spot for her. It was too bad Eri was angry with her. Of course, if anyone had a right to be angry, it was probably him. After all, he was the one who lost a girlfriend. But he wasn't. No real reason why. His anger was complexly channeled where it belonged—against S.I.U.

"I'm really sorry about all this," Helena said again.

"Now that you know the full story, just be careful what you say. I'm sure it will all blow over eventually. To be honest, Eri just needs to see if the two of you can handle yourselves. She's a tough girl. She respects women who can hold their own." Myers patted

Helena's back once and then opened the diner door for her.

The air-conditioning felt great after being cooped up in stale limo air for so long. The team found a faded brown booth in the corner of the dive. A waitress dressed in a lemon yellow uniform handed them sticky menus with the promise of returning soon.

"So, what does one eat in these places?" Helena asked, looking over the menu.

"Anything but chili," Charlie joked.

Eri shot him a look.

"What? We have to share space, so chili is not a good idea."

He had a point. Myers glanced at the pictures of food and decided on fried chicken in a basket with an upgrade to onion rings.

The rest of the group mostly got hamburgers and fries, topped off with milkshakes. Not that anyone could blame them. They had been eating canned food for almost two weeks now. A little grease might do them some good.

The waitress returned with their orders. It didn't take long for them to devour their food. As she walked away, the hairs on Myers neck stood up. Two booths away, a man who clearly didn't belong in a trucker's diner, peered their way. He had on dark glasses, his hair was slicked back, and he wore a designer black button-down shirt and vest. A suit jacket lay on the table next to him. Though he had a newspaper, it was obvious it wasn't his main focus.

Myers pulled out his pistol under the table and made eye contact with Laura.

Her gaze dropped to his gun and then to what had

pulled his attention. Instantly, she followed suit. Like a game of follow the leader, each person slowly, without making it too obvious prepared themselves for the worst.

The man got up, wrapped a coat over his arm, and exited the diner.

Laura raised her hand to the waitress. "I'm so sorry, but we have an emergency. Can we get all this to go?"

"Oh, my, I hope nothing serious." The women waddled quickly to the kitchen and returned with Styrofoam containers. Everyone busied themselves with packing their food, while also keeping one eye on the door and windows.

"Ready?" Laura said.

"We can't have these bags in our hands, Laura," Bryce said.

"Give all the food to Helena and Alicia. They can leave after us, after we know it is safe." Laura motioned for them to sit at the booth by the door, but away from the window.

The ladies quickly obeyed.

The rest readied their guns and walked toward the exit. Laura glanced back at them and then walked out the door. Adrenaline pumped through Myers' body. He prayed it was just one guy. Of course, that one guy could reveal their location. The mysterious man had to be taken out. Bryce stepped out next. Then Eri. Then Charlie. Myers would take up the rear. Since there wasn't shooting already, chances are the enemy would likely start when the last person left. Myers readied himself with a deep breath and then walked out. The lot was empty. A warm breeze blew leaves along the ground. Crows cawed in the trees above. His team surrounded the limo, looking each way, all wide-eyed and alert.

Charlie got in the driver's seat and started the engine.

Myers ducked back in and yelled for the girls to run to the limo with him.

They ran out and ducked in the open back door.

"Everyone in," Laura commanded.

One-by-one, they piled in. Eri got in the passenger's seat. Bryce in back. Laura stepped in last and slammed the door.

All eyes shared the trepidation Myers was feeling. Sure, they made it to the car, but did that really mean anything? Were they hyper sensitive, or was there a real concern? Was he a scout and just reported back he had found us? No one could know for sure.

"We need to find him. We shouldn't be in here?" Charlie said, turning off the engine.

"Fine. Bryce and I will go." Laura opened the door and stepped to the pavement, and her husband followed. She leaned into the passenger side. "Drive down the road and see what you see, then come back and get us in about fifteen minutes around the corner by that gas station we saw earlier."

She slammed the door, and they ran off.

"You girls look out the side windows and see if you see anything," Myers said.

Charlie stepped on the gas, and they rolled down the desert road. Myers leaned through the opening by the driver. The orange and brown landscape was filled with empty warehouses and run-down buildings. The area seemed vacant and empty. If this person drove away, there would have to be some sort of dust cloud behind the car until they pulled onto the main road. They were only a few minutes behind him.

"He could be hiding in one of these shells," Myers said.

"I don't see any fresh dust or cars," Eri said.

"There!" Helena said from the back seat.

Myers jumped next to her. A haze of dirt hovered next to an old train station on the left side the road a few blocks down.

Charlie did a U-turn, sending Myers and the girls hard against the left side of the car. "Sorry."

Myers righted himself and checked his gun. "What's the plan?"

"Maybe we check it out and send Helena back to get Laura and Bryce," Eri said. It wasn't said, but it was implied to make Helena useful.

"I like that," Charlie said.

Myers peered at Helena. "Are you good with that?"

She nodded.

Charlie pulled over about a block away. "Helena, it's all yours."

Chapter Twenty-One

Eri hoped Helena could handle this. Not that driving a car was hard; Eri just didn't trust her. The girl had already sold them out once. And not to forget, Alicia was found with Greenstone. They were lucky Eri had a conscience.

The team exited the vehicle. Alicia got in the passenger seat next to Helena, and they drove away.

"What now?" Eri said.

"Come on." Myers waved for them to run from building to building, until reaching the edge of the train station.

The wooden buildings were rotting from abandonment—termite ridden, peeling paint. The windows were boarded up or broken out. This area appeared forgotten. All the more reason those people shouldn't be here. Myers pointed two fingers at his eyes and then pointed for Charlie to go high and Eri to go right.

Charlie nodded and took off to get on top of the parked train.

Myers shuffled forward.

Eri ducked behind the train station, gun held in both hands. She circled around the side and knelt under a window. There were two people talking inside. Inching forward, she tried to get a better idea of what they were saying.

"I think we can assume he'll pay for it," the one man said.

The other man twirled a toothpick in his mouth. "I think we need to find a better buyer."

It wasn't him. *Oh no!* Her heart sank. She ran around the building, almost crashing into Myers. "It's not the guy. We have to go back."

Myers nodded andwaved to Charlie.

He leapt down and joined them. "It's not him."

They both nodded.

"We have no choice, we have to run. Laura and Bryce could be in danger." Eri took off sprinting, and the guys joined her. Within blocks, they were all wheezing. This was a simple reminder they had to exercise more. The time spent in the mountains should have been time spent training and getting stronger. Years of martial arts training had taught her the importance of that.

They passed several more abandoned buildings; finally, the limo came into sight. The two girls were not there. Laura and Bryce were also not in sight.

"Where is everybody?" Eri said, panicked.

"I don't know. Split up," Myers said. "Meet back at the limo."

Each went in a different direction. Eri sprinted toward the back of the trucker's diner where a row of semis stood parked. Her heart froze. The man with glasses—it was him locking the back of a truck closed. Energy coursed through her veins. She had to figure out what to do. What if Laura and Bryce were locked in there?

She ducked behind a truck next to it and slinked forward, keeping her eye on his location. A stocky man with red hair and a handlebar mustache stepped down from the truck. Glasses man handed him a black duffle bag, most likely carrying money. The driver tossed it across the cab, shook his hand, and jumped into the semi.

Oh no. What if he was leaving? There were only seconds. What to do? Eri hurried to the back of the semi. It held a large lock with combination. She glanced back around the truck. Glasses guy had walked away. Eri stepped up on the back of the truck, knocked lightly, and then put her ear to the back of the truck.

"What are you doing?" Laura's voice said from behind her.

Eri was confused for a moment and then jumped down. She rushed to her friend and hugged her.

Laura laughed. "What's going on?"

"The guy with glasses paid this driver. I thought you were locked inside."

"Yeah, we've been watching the exchange. I don't think he was here for us. I think he was suspicious, because whatever is in there is likely not legal. I think he was making sure we weren't a threat." Laura patted her arm. "Sorry, if we scared you. Are you okay? You seem flushed."

"We ran all the way back." Eri glanced around. "Where are the girls?"

"I thought they were with you."

The truck started up, and then Eri heard it. Screaming. Banging. One clearly Alicia's high pitch voice.

Laura's eyes went wide.

The truck—they were on the truck. But why? Though Eri didn't think they should have been asked on this adventure, she also didn't want to see them suffer. "What do we do?"

"We follow it. Grab everyone. Let's move."

They both ran off. Eri sprinted for the limo, grabbing Charlie and Myers on the way. "No time to explain. There is a semi in this lot that is about to leave with Helena and Alicia inside. We have to follow it."

Color red filled Myers face. He took off for the driver's side. Laura and Bryce came flying up and jumped in. Charlie and Eri both got in the front.

"There it is," Laura said, pointing to the burgundy cab and trailer just pulling out of the lot. "Why would they take them and not us? I don't get it."

Eri bit her lip. Did she say what she was thinking? This happened all the time in Chinatown. It was the reason her uncle was so strict. "I think I know."

Laura leaned forward through the glass. "What?"

"I think…" Eri took a large breath and slowly pushed it out. "I think its white slavery."

"But they aren't white." Myers seemed confused.

Laura laughed. "No, that means the sex trade."

"What?!?" Myers swerved. Charlie touched his arm. Myers corrected the car. "Why do you think that?"

"Many girls went missing in Chinatown all the time. Some showed back up as prostitutes." Eri sighed. "People don't take young girls for nothing. A fifteen-year-old on the black market is huge. I think we're following a trafficking truck."

"This is America. Surely, that sort of stuff doesn't—" Myers started.

"Really, Myers, you don't think kidnapping children for personal gain doesn't happen here," Eri said sarcastically. "Unfortunately, it happens more than you know—to millions every year. We think we had it bad because we were kidnapped to kill people. What is about to happen to Helena and Alicia is vile, the worst kind of evil. I know what happens inside those brothels." Eri shuddered at the memory of accidently walking into one once. Her voice cracked, "No person should ever have to endure the torture."

The car fell quiet.

Eri's belly churned. The few bites of food she had consumed threatened to come back up. Closing her eyes, she willed her stomach to calm. All the anger she felt for those girls was now channeled into getting them back. Laura was right. They were part of their family now. The only reason they were caught was because she sent them back to get Laura.

"So, when that guy was watching our table, he wasn't looking at us. He was checking out the girls," Charlie said carefully.

"It seems so." Eri laid her head against the window and closed her eyes. Where would this truck take them? Though they tried to avoid being shot at, they were driving into a very lucrative business that would not give these girls up without a fight.

"Don't follow too closely," Laura said into the opening at one point.

After a few hours, the car slowed down. Eri opened her eyes and glanced around. It seemed they were in an industrial area just outside Salt Lake City.

"These guys have guts to do this right under the Mormon's noses," Charlie said. "That's bold."

"Seriously." Bryce laughed.

The truck pulled into a shipping dock.

Myers parked the car a few yards away behind a

row of dumpsters. "Now what?"

Eri sat up. "This is not going to be easy. You know that, right?"

"I just hope we have enough ammo." Laura checked her gun. "We need to catch him off guard. Bryce and I will go scope out the building, so we don't have any surprises. Myers, Charlie, and Eri—get the girls."

They had their orders. Each moved toward them.

The man came around and unlocked the back of the truck. Eri round kicked him in the face. He stumbled back, dazed. She punched again, and he landed to the pavement. Myers stepped into the truck. Two men with guns came out. Eri and Charlie ducked behind the truck and fired back. Laura and Bryce shot them from behind.

Both crumpled.

Laura and Bryce darted back inside.

"I need help in here," Myers said. His voice indicated a problem.

They peeked in, and instantly, Eri wanted to cry.

There had to be over twenty girls blindfolded, gagged, and tied up. "What do we do?" Charlie said.

"We free them. Come on." Eri used Charlie's shoulder to get up into the tall bed.

More gunfire sounded from inside the building. She prayed her friends were okay.

One-by-one, they removed the ladies bindings. Fear permeated the space. Each girl obviously didn't realize they were being rescued. In many languages, they pleaded. Myers helped them down to the ground to meet Charlie.

Helena and Alicia were in the back. They jumped up and hugged Eri, weeping. Any problem she had with them, it was gone. She was glad they were safe.

"Are you okay?" she asked, pulling back.

"No one touched us yet," Helena said.

Eri helped Alicia to the ground and turned back, surprised.

Myers leaned back from a hug with Helena and brought his lips to hers. They were kissing. That was unexpected.

Eri turned away and motioned for Charlie to help her down. His gaze went past her to the couple in the truck. An amused grin fell on his face. He winked. Eri grabbed his chin and brought his lips to hers. He kissed her back and smiled.

Myers and Helena joined them on the ground.

Women were huddled, confused, blinded by the bright light. What did they do with them? "Now what?" Eri said. It seemed to be her mantra of the day.

Laura and Bryce entered covered in splatters of blood. Bryce grasped the side of his arm.

"Are you hurt?" Eri asked.

"I'll be okay." He winced as he slid off the loading dock to the ground.

"Let me see." Eri slid up his T-shirt in back. Blood seeped from a stab wound. "You need to dress that before it becomes an issue."

"I can do it," Alicia said. "I've done stitches for my dad before. And Laura brought the sewing kit from the attic."

Bryce nodded and followed Alicia to the car.

"How bad was it in there?" Eri asked Laura.

"Pretty bad," Laura said. "There are more girls in the basement. We freed them, but they aren't leaving. Eri, Helena, and I should go back down. Keep your guns hidden. I think they are extremely scared."

"But what about them?" Charlie asked to the women standing to his left.

"Charlie, take them down the road to that fast food place. Get them some water and something to eat. Have them use the phone."

He nodded. Together, Charlie tried to corral them.

The women turned for the building. "Myers, keep watch," Laura said. "Helena, I cannot prepare you for the bloodbath that is inside there. Are you sure you're okay to help? If not, I won't be upset. You can stay out here."

She shook her head, her ponytail bobbing side to side. "No, please, I want to help. What those girls went through could have been me. I'll be fine."

Laura led them through the warehouse quickly. Dozens of lifeless bodies lay in pools of blood across the cement floor. At the heart of the carnage stood a wooden table, shattered computer monitors and equipment clinging to its splintered shell. A lone human figure cradled the table at its edge. A thick stream of red seeped into the wood from his neck.

They walked to a cold, steel door, down a flight of stairs. A strong smell of mildew permeated the hall to the bottom. Dirty, stained two-inch mattresses littered the floor. A group of women huddled, half-naked against the back of the room. Some yelled curse words. Some pleas. Others chattered in nervous conversation.

No one could look at this and not be affected. Eri's heart ached for these women and what they had been through. The animals that would trade a soul for money was unreal. Every inch of her five-foot-three frame wanted to kill someone for this. But Laura had done it already. No wonder they won. All this rage, any person could win.

Laura eased her hands out in front of her, patting the air softly, in an effort to assure they came in peace.

Eri and Helena followed suit.

"We are not here to hurt you. We've come to rescue you," Laura said.

"You have to go! They will kill us if we talk to you," one woman said.

Eri shook her head. "They are all dead. Just look at my friend."

"I killed all of them." Laura glanced down and wiped her hand against her sleeve, mixing the still wet blood from her hand into the weave of her black jacket.

Another woman stood clinching her robe. "Are you the police?"

"No, we're, um, secret agents," Eri said. She wasn't sure where that came from, but it was better than the truth—that they were on the run for their lives, because they left their own form of slavery. That would only make them afraid to leave. "Come on, let's get you out of here."

"There are others. They could find us," one said. "What have you done?"

"We will make you disappear; they won't be able to find you," Laura said.

"She's very good at that," Eri said.

"Are you sure it is safe?" a lady asked.

Eri reached to her. The girl pulled back, her muscles tensed. Eri eased away. "Sorry. I promise. It is safe." Eri traced the room with her eyes. A box of clothes and sheets sat clumsily upon crooked shelving. She slid it from its place and gifted the girls with blankets and jackets.

Laura turned toward the hallway. "Time to move."

They stepped swiftly back through the office rooms, a newly formed graveyard. As they passed, Eri noticed track marks, bruises, and signs of malnutrition. Some looked worse than others, but each had a sad story. She counted thirty-two. Her heart was so heavy she thought it might erupt. Eri followed the last girl out. "Look straight ahead. Walk quickly. There are a lot of dead bad guys."

The women did not obey. They stopped to spit at the bodies. Or yell some expletive. One woman even kicked a corpse. Each took her time to see the carnage Laura and Bryce had caused. A sense of retribution filled the air, as the women paraded through the lifeless souls that had caused them so much pain. Finally, they made it to the opening in the warehouse. Each squinted and covered their eyes.

One woman said, "I haven't seen the sun in five years."

Another said, "Seven."

She couldn't be more than eighteen. Once again, Eri felt punched in the gut. This wasn't right. The emotion she felt could not be consoled.

They moved them out and toward the fast food place to meet with the rest of the girls.

Laura came back and whispered in Eri's ear. "We need to call the cops and then disappear."

"Agreed," Eri said.

Once they all were inside, holding a cup of water and sharing plates of fries, Laura pulled the manager of the restaurant aside. "You need to call 9-1-1. Tell them that fifty survivors of a trafficking ring just crashed your establishment. They can take it from there."

The young man's eyes went wide, but he listened and walked to the back.

Laura motioned for her team to head for an exit.

Outside, they found the limo and piled in.

"A good deed done," Charlie said. "Feels really good."

Eri agreed. To have rescued so many people—it felt amazing. Who knew, maybe they found a new career that fit their skills.

Chapter Twenty-Two

Myers sat in the back of the limo, afraid to look at Helena next to him. He had been so excited she was okay that he kissed her. Now he felt stupid. His heart still belonged to Denise. He had no right to kiss another girl. Playing with a girl's emotions was the old Myers. The vow to change had come with the new life. And this is worse, because he had to see Helena every day. At some point, they would have to talk. He just prayed she didn't hate him.

"We should be crossing over into Colorado in a few minutes," Bryce said.

Everyone leaned forward to see out the front. Though this vehicle fit them all, it wasn't the best for this sort of thing. A wooden sign that read, "Welcome to Colorful Colorado" hung by the side of the road. Beyond it were flat lands, as well as some mountains. Everyone cheered as they drove past the state line.

Helena glanced at him and smiled.

He offered an awkward, fake grin and then sat back to stare out the window. The feeling of being watched remained. He was sure she stared at him, wondering, curious, afraid. Nothing could happen. And in this moment, he could not even reassure her. Too many ears. It would have to wait.

When they hit the Kansas border, everyone cheered again, followed by complaints for rest, bathrooms, and food. They pulled into a gas station complete with bathroom and snack shop. The lot piled out and dispersed. Helena hung back, obviously wanting to catch Myers alone. Though all he wanted was a chocolate bar with some kind of nut, he would have to get this over with. He faced her and willed himself to stare into her eyes. The softness of her eyes reminded him of an anime cartoon. "I shouldn't have kissed you." He shoved his hands in his pants and turned to go.

She caught his arm and turned him back. "Why not?"

He sucked in his bottom lip and exhaled through his nose. "Because, I am still in love with someone else."

"Denise?"

Hearing her voice deepened the knife of guilt. "Yes."

"Then I'm sorry too."

He raised an eyebrow.

"I don't mean to disrespect her or you. I'm here when you're ready." She offered a closed mouth smile and strode briskly to the store.

Myers stared after her, not sure what just happened. He'd analyze it later. Right now, he needed a large soda and sugar. Inside the store, everyone filled his or her arms with junk and the occasional good food. Laura made sure lots of water was also in the purchase. Myers hoped their money still held out. He never asked how much Helena had given for this trip.

Outside, he relished in the smoothness of the candy bar. The caramel nougat and peanuts topped with chocolate made him smile. There was no secret he loved candy. His computer station at home used to be surrounded by wrappers. In a plastic bag, he also had string cheese and an apple. Laura had made sure he ate something healthy. *Probably a good idea.* He grinned.

He downed the bar with a liter of cola. His stomach rebelled, and he burped, just as Eri walked in front of him.

"Gross, Myers."

"Hey, better this way, my dear." He winked.

"Gross," she said again.

He laughed. His mind flashed to Denise pretending to be grossed out by his burping, until one day she showed him up. His heart ached for his best friend. The way she sassed him about everything. No person had ever been able to get under his skin and then make him love them, like she did. Her punked-out hair and sparkling eyes—Denise's memory fresh as it was before he lost her. With all the running and mission, he had not allowed himself to grieve.

A sudden wave of sadness washed over him. Deep and besieging, he shot around the building, folded to the ground, and sobbed. His entire body shook, convulsing. Tears poured like hard rain to the dirt below. Sounds of torment from his throat caught to his ears. He tried to soften them, as to not bring anyone to see him in this state.

A hand wrapped around his shoulder and held him. He didn't know the owner. Nor did he care. He sensed others came, and the person holding him held them back. His head pounded, hot and wet. He could hardly breathe from the running nose. He lifted his head slowly. Helena.

She held a wad of toilet paper out to him. Someone must have grabbed it for her. He took it and squeaked out, "Thanks." Almost embarrassed, he stood, wiping at his face. He blew his nose and breathed deep. Numbness enveloped his body. His eyes burned, and his head ached. But through all the physicality of what he just put himself through, a weight had been lifted. He had allowed himself to grieve. His eyes met Helena's. "Thank you."

"That's what friends are for." She smiled and withdrew a tear on his cheek. "Come on. Let's get back. Everyone is waiting."

He rolled his shoulders back and tried to compose himself. "I think I need to stop by the restroom first. I'll meet you back at the car." Without looking at the group, he went straight for the men's room. He splashed water on his face and glanced in the scratched-up mirror. His eyes were swollen and red, his dark face splotchy, puffy. The green hue of the bathroom fluorescents made him look even worse.

Charlie opened the door and came behind him in the mirror. "You okay, man?"

"Just needed to get it out."

Charlie nodded. "Anything I can do?"

"Not make a big deal out of it."

He nodded again.

They walked back to the car. The sun had just begun to set on the horizon. The descending colors mirrored his heart. A chapter closing—a love lost. His gaze traveled to Helena, who smiled with concern. It was not dawn, but he now knew he had a friend to walk with him. He smiled back and climbed in next to her, at peace.

****

By noon the next day, they had reached Maryland.

The cheers were more somber this time. The reality that they were minutes away from the monsters who killed the people they loved was evident in the expressions around the limo. The choice of car was suddenly apropos. A limousine here in Washington D.C. blended in. Luckily, they managed to get here without any bullet holes.

Myers stared out the side window at the landscape. The city was wall-to-wall brick tenements and office buildings. Some varied in color. Most worn and disheveled. How is it so poor here? In his mind, this area should be filled with rich businessmen and senators. The people who made a difference were just around the bend. Yet, the outskirts seemed deprived and forgotten. How did the world's government exist in this backyard and not get involved?

"What now?" Charlie had his nose pressed against the window, both hands flattened against the pane. "We can't just go up and ring the bell."

Bryce pulled the long car into an alleyway and shut off the engine. Laura and he joined them in the back.

"Charlie, log into the file. We need to figure out more intel first," Laura said.

Charlie withdrew his laptop and started clicking the mouse.

"What do we know?" Myers asked, agitated. The idea of coming without a plan and now sitting here without one, for some reason, upset him. He tried to calm himself with a few deep breaths.

"We know they operate out of D.C. and that Harding is a key player." Laura unfolded a map of the area and placed it in the middle of them. Each person leaned in, not really knowing what they were seeing.

"Do we know where *they* are?" Eri asked.

Charlie glanced up over his laptop and smiled. "We do now." He pushed forward, grabbed the highlighter from Laura's hand, popped the lid off using his mouth, and circled a location on the map. "Here. That's S.I.U."

"You're sure," Laura asked.

Charlie recapped the marker and handed it back. He then turned his laptop around so everyone could see the schematics of a property. "This is the blueprint of their organization's headquarters. The address is even listed."

"That was mighty nice of them," Myers said.

"Yes, agreed, and so dumb." Charlie smiled. "So, now we know where and what; we need the *how*."

Myers chewed his lip. What did they do? "We don't really have enough ammo and supplies to be effective. We need to go shopping."

"We need a place to stay," Bryce said. "It gets super cold here this time of year, so the car is out. And this cannot happen overnight. Being reckless will get us killed."

Laura nodded. "I agree. We need a place. Ideas?"

Nobody spoke. It was the same internal argument they had at each stop. Could they get what they needed without hurting or stealing? Usually, the answer was no. That response wore on each of them. No one wanted to be a thief. It was by necessity. The better question should be *what could they do that was legal*?

"Could we clear out a portion of a crack house?" Myers circled with his pointer finger a portion on the map that appeared to be a grouping of low-income housing. "I had a roommate in jail who once talked about this place. They found him in an alleyway in

Orange County, stoned, but was in jail for holding. He had said he missed D.C., because there were lots of old tenements the owners abandoned, and drug addicts could squat there without the worry of cops."

"I've heard of that too," Charlie said.

"Wouldn't that be dangerous?" Helena asked.

"Not if we clean it out." Myers held up his gun and winked.

Laura glanced at Bryce. "What do you think?"

"I think we need a place to stay. Can't afford to get a real place, and we are out of options."

"It's settled then. Let's find us a crack house," Laura said.

Chapter Twenty-Three

Laura purchased three disposable cell phones and passed them out to the three groups. Bryce would go with her. Charlie and Eri would go together; Myers, Helena, and Alicia would take up the rear. They were simply to report what they saw, not move on anything by themselves.

A bitter chill brushed against them. Laura pulled her leather jacket tighter, trying to retain body heat. The heavy air hugged them with a sign that winter was quickly closing in. Her breath was visible as she spoke, "Back at the limo in one hour. If you see something we really need, call." Laura stuffed her phone in the back of her black jeans, checked her weapon, and nodded. "One hour."

The three teams split.

A tall gray and pink building lay to their left. Bryce and Laura cut across the busy street and went inside. Loud bass resonated from above. Graffiti decorated the walls, and trash littered the stairs. The smell of urine permeated her nose. Laura touched the gun in her waistband as they climbed the stairs. Each step creaked in annoyance.

They climbed to the top. Several doors lay open. Only one was closed at the end. One-by-one, they peeked inside the rooms. Most still had residents or things too grotesque to consider. Bryce examined the last door on the right and motioned with his head for Laura do the same.

There were old mattresses on the floor and more graffiti on the walls. A small kitchenette lay at the back with burned foil and white residue. A slight toxic smell of burning plastic mixed with more urine hung heavy in the room. "It isn't much, but it could work with a little effort."

"And how do we know the owners aren't just away?" Bryce asked.

"We don't. But we're armed." She tried the door handle. It was unlocked. She shut it.

"And the smell?" She just noticed Bryce had a bandana around his face.

"I have some tricks." She winked. "Shall we check in with the group?"

He nodded. "Sounds good."

When they reached the limo, a couple young Hispanic guys dressed in hoodies were peering into the side windows. Laura smirked. They had no idea who they were messing with. "Can I help you?"

One saddled up to her, speaking in a heavy accent. "Hola, Chiquita, looks to me like your boyfriend just bought us a new limousine, complete with a beautiful girl to go inside."

"I suggest you back up and run away," Bryce said.

"No, homes, you back up. Me and the lady, we're taking this limo."

"Is that so?" Bryce crossed his arms, clearly amused.

"Yeah, that's so." The kid grabbed Laura's arm.

Laura cranked his arm backward. The guy screamed out in pain. She pushed him off, and he landed hard against the limo. Another kid rushed her. She dropped him with a kick to the chest. "You done?"

The first guy got up and tried to swing, but she blocked it and punched him in the jaw, sending him to ground.

"Stay," she said.

The fire in his eyes said he wasn't done yet.

Bryce shook his head and stepped back, smirking.

The two guys rushed her. She blocked their advances, kicked one in the face, and punched the other in the side, then did the same to the other. Both were on the ground hugging injuries when Eri and Charlie walked up.

"What's going on?" Charlie said.

"They thought they could kidnap Laura and steal our wheels," Bryce said amused.

Eri and Charlie laughed.

The boys slowly got up, nursing their wounds. "Who are you?" the boy who had originally talked to them asked.

"I tried to warn you, kid," Bryce said. "I'd tell your friends this limo is off limits, comprende?"

"Let's get out of here," the other kids said. "She's loco."

"Got that right." Bryce grinned.

The boys backed up and then ran off.

"How was your workout, dear," Bryce joked as he kissed her cheek.

Myers, Helena, and Alicia ran up.

"What did we miss," Myers asked.

"Laura kicking booty," Charlie said.

Myers batted the air. "Awe, that old routine."

They all laughed.

"Okay, what did we find?" Laura asked.

Myers's group didn't find much. Charlie and Eri said the one they found might have too many holes to keep them warm. Bryce shared their find, and the team agreed to go check it out.

They sauntered back to the tenement, up the stairs, and to the end of the hall. The door was ajar. Laura reached for her gun, touched her lips, and nodded. Everyone reached for their guns and slowed their steps. They inched forward in unison, trying hard not to make any noise. It was hard with the creaky old floor.

Laura reached there first. She peeked inside. A haggard young woman, probably in her late twenties, stood over the stove. Laura put her gun behind her back with her left hand and rapped on the door with her right. "Excuse me."

The women flipped around, eyes wide.

"Is this your place?"

Her mouth dropped open, but nothing escaped. Fear resonated from every part of her shaky demeanor.

"Do you live here?" Laura tried again.

The woman shook her head and shuffled to the door. As she passed Charlie, he asked, "Does anyone else live here?"

She shook her head, maneuvered around them, out the door, and into a run.

The team glanced around the space.

"It's functional, but needs a lot of work," Eri said.

"Yeah, especially the smell of crack and pee." Myers grimaced.

Helena had a hand over her mouth and nose. "Is that what that smell is? Gross."

"Bryce, Helena, and Alicia will get the stuff from

our limo and work to fix this up," Laura said. "Why don't the rest of you go buy some supplies?"

"Are we talking hardware or domestic?" Myers asked.

"Domestic for now." Laura handed them some money. "Be careful. This neighborhood is—"

They nodded. "We got it," Charlie said.

Each of them departed to their task. Laura and Bryce busied themselves bringing stuff from the car, while the girls started on cleaning the room. There was no electricity, but luckily, there was running water and a gas stove. Most likely a few people still lived in the building, but most of it had been abandoned.

Around midnight, the place seemed almost livable. The walls and kitchenette had been scrubbed in bleach. The graffiti was gone. The floor was now littered with scented candles, and the aroma from a pot of stew cooking in the kitchenette helped fill the room with pleasant smells. Sleeping bags and blankets littered the floor, each holding a member of the group as they sat in a circle discussing their next plan.

"I think we need to find a way to get equipment," Laura said.

"Yeah, but what do we need?" Myers asked.

Charlie held up a hand. "Look, we need a plan, before we can buy. You know I'm resourceful, but first, I have to know what's up."

Myers shook his head. "I can steal us anything. I just need to know what I'm boosting."

Laura tossed out copies of the blueprint Charlie had copied at the liquor store. "Here is their building, but I don't think breaking in will take them down. We need to know where they'll hurt. Anything, Charlie?"

"I can access their funds, assuming they haven't changed anything since we broke into the dummy company." Charlie clicked a few keys on the laptop.

"Funds are good," Eri said.

"Not enough," Laura said. "What else?"

"We could go after Harding," Bryce said.

Laura had thought of that. It probably was the right idea, just not one she was quick to approve. He was her friend. At one point, he helped them. Then hurt them. It was likely he shot Julio and kidnapped Alicia. He probably ordered the hit on Denise. Why they were such a threat to him, she did not know. But he had their number and intended them harm. He had to go.

"Okay, collect intel on Harding. However, we've seen that taking out the leader is not enough. We'll start there, but we'll need more. Charlie, keep working on that." She stood to put her cup of barely touched stew on the counter. "In the meantime, we should probably try to get some sleep. We'll figure the rest out in the morning."

Around the room, candles blew out. One was left by the door, where Eri had first watch.

Chapter Twenty-Four

Eri watched as everyone blew out his or her candles. Only hers still remained. The room smelled of vanilla and lavender—a wonderful change from the original urinal smell. Though she couldn't at the moment, she desperately wanted to close her eyes in the dim light. After all the traveling and walking today, her body ached desperately for some rest. She agreed to take first watch, because once she was asleep, it would be like death. This way, she could get her turn out of the way. Not that she minded much.

To some extent, being on duty was exhilarating and watching others sleep slightly amusing. Almost instantly, snores permeated from Myers's direction. The man could give a grizzly bear a run for its money. Charlie was her favorite to watch. His long strands of hair fell over his face. His chiseled jaw relaxed and looked at peace. Once she allowed herself to open her heart to him, it was amazing how fast she fell. Though the words had not escaped her mouth, she did love him.

A noise stirred in the hall. The hairs on her neck spiked. She inched forward, bent to the floor, but on her feet, and put her ear to the door. Shuffling. Rattling. Door open. Door closed.

Eri sat back. False alarm. She tore open a bag of peanut butter pretzels and popped one in her mouth. Her chewing seemed thunderous in the still air of sleepers. Maybe she should chew slower.

One of Charlie's eyes opened. He smiled.

"Sorry," she whispered and pushed the bag away.

"Mind if I join you?"

"Did my crunching wake you?"

"No." He laughed. "I just can't sleep." He dropped his hand in the bag, withdrew a pretzel, and popped it in his mouth. The crunching was loud, as he didn't try to mask it.

"Aren't you next shift?"

He nodded. "Sure, but I can just do yours with you, and then when you sleep, I'll do mine."

She smiled, grateful. Maybe now she could stay awake.

He slid next to her, leaned his head against the wall, and took her hand in his. His fingers caressed hers, sending shock waves throughout her body. He faced her with his head still resting on the wall. She followed suit. The two of them stared at each other. His eyes drew her in. How she wanted to kiss him. Was it appropriate in this setting? He inched closer. Her heart pounded. Energy heated the space between them. Luring her. Slowly, their lips met. Soft, moist, hot. Passion pulsated through her. He wrapped his arms around her, drawing them together. Slowly, she laid back and he followed her down.

A slight movement at the door.

They both sat up.

Charlie held a finger to his lips.

Eri readied her gun.

The handle turned, but didn't budge from the makeshift lock they had created. The person on the other side stood there for a good minute, before trying the knob again. This time, he or she shuffled away.

Eri and Charlie relaxed.

"Where were we?" Charlie smiled, holding his hand out to her.

"I'd better behave." Eri slid back a foot from him, but smiled.

He scooted next to her and took her hand in his. "Okay, but it isn't going to be easy."

She had to agree. Every pore cried out to ignore her conscience and just make out with this man. But she would be smart. Instead, they talked about random stuff. Finally, her shift was up. She kissed him goodnight and crawled in between the blankets. It didn't take but a few minutes for her to drift off to sleep.

****

When Eri opened her eyes, the first face she saw was Charlie's. His gaze was on her. He grinned. "Good morning, beautiful."

"What time is it?" she croaked.

He glanced at his watch. "Just after eight."

She slid up and glanced around the room. Everyone was still asleep. "Shouldn't someone be on duty?"

"Myers was until a few minutes ago. I told him I could take it again. Hungry?"

"Starving."

He stood and offered a hand up. "How about I take you to breakfast?"

Eri raked fingers through her hair, trying to smooth her tousled tresses. "We can't just go out. What if we are seen?"

"We were all over the place yesterday. It'll be fine. I'll leave a note." Charlie grabbed a cardboard leftover from the bottom of a candy bar, scribbled some words, and then turned to her. "We're clear. Come on."

"The door will be unlocked."

Charlie nodded and tapped Myers.

Myers grunted.

"Dude, lock the door when I leave."

Myers grunted again and rolled over.

Charlie grabbed Eri's hand and led her down the stairs to the lobby below. Outside, the sun was attempting to shine; the air was cold, crisp, and clear. Few people lined the streets. A donut and coffee shop was just a block away. They walked toward it holding hands, talking and laughing. It almost felt normal. *A real girlfriend and boyfriend going to get breakfast.* She grinned. It might be a small fantasy, but it sent joy through her being to just be teenagers on a date for a moment.

Charlie held the door open for her, and she walked in. The aroma of brewed coffee, maple, chocolate, and fresh baked donuts wafted to her nose. She inhaled and smiled. Her stomach rumbled. She was hungrier than she realized. They walked to the counter. Charlie ordered an apple fritter and a large coffee. Eri asked for a maple twist and a hot tea. They paid and moved to a small table in the corner.

"We should probably order a box to take back," Eri said, ripping a piece off her donut and popping it in her mouth. It was soft, sweet, and luxurious. It had been a while since she had had one. "Do you think our lives could ever be like this?"

"Like what?" Charlie asked, wiping sugar from his top lip.

"You and I, just going on a date whenever we

want. Not worrying about who is watching us or if we're safe."

He reached across the table and wrapped his hand around hers. His blue eyes peeked through strands of blond bangs, his mouth serious. "I promise. I will help make that happen for us someday."

Her pulse raced, especially at the word *us*. So much emotion filled her heart. "Would it be crazy or too soon to say I love you?"

He brought her hand to his lips and beamed. "Dear, I think we loved each other months ago. We were just slow in acting on it."

She leaned across the table and kissed his cheek. "Agreed."

Charlie slid his hand back, letting go of her hand, so he could put sugar in his coffee.

Eri took a sip of her tea and then ripped another soft piece from her donut. As she took her last bite, dread slammed against her chest. *Please, no.* Eri's eyes focused on a group of men in black entering the building down the block.

Charlie followed her gaze. "What is it?"

"Men just entered our place."

"What?!?"

Without more conversation, they jumped up from the table and started to the entrance.

Panic rose in Eri's throat. "We left the door unlocked."

They sprinted out the front door and down the street. Once inside the tenement, they withdrew their guns and slowed their pace. Eri listened to see where they might be. Keeping their backs against the wall, both of them inched up the stairs slowly. Each step creaked in betrayal. Eri squeezed her eyes shut and tried to move without weight. Not easy, but the step was less noisy. At the top of the stairs, Eri peeked around the corner. Three men stood at their door. One of them tried the handle. Each exchanged glances. It was locked. Eri exhaled in relief. Myers had done what they asked.

Eri remembered they had phones. "Call them," she whispered.

Charlie nodded. He dialed and stepped back down the stairwell. Eri remained watching, waiting.

One of the men knocked.

No answer.

Charlie came back up the steps, still holding the phone to his ear. "Get ready. On the count of three, we're hitting from this side, and Laura and them are ready on the other side." He whispered in the phone. "One, two, three…"

They rushed the hall with their guns. The door sprang open with more guns. The men dropped their one gun, hands raised, expressions mixed with surprise and frustration.

"Who are you?" Laura said, reaching for the men's one gun.

A man with greased back hair and an anchor goatee tightened his lips like he was sucking on a lemon. "Who are we? Who are you?" he asked in a thick Italian accent. "This is our place."

Laura glanced at Eri and back to the men. "We didn't know. We needed a place to crash last night. Not trying to cause any trouble."

The three men exchanged glances. Then goatee said, "I'll tell you what. You let us have what we came for, and you can stay here as long as you want."

"Whatever you want." Laura stepped back, allowing him to enter.

The other two men motioned to follow, but Laura blocked them.

Eri walked over to where they were and watched as goatee walked to the wall by the stove and pushed. A panel opened, and a black bag dropped out. He grabbed it, tucked it in his lapel, pushed the panel closed, and strode back to his men. Before exiting, he turned to Laura and said, "If you get in my way, I will bury you."

Laura placed her weapon in her waistband and handed the man his gun back. "I am not here for you, sir. Our group has other fish to fry."

This seemed to intrigue the man. He faced her, an eyebrow raised. "Are you cops?"

Charlie laughed. "Hardly."

All eyes shot to him. He held up his hands. "Sorry."

"Not even close," Laura said. "It's a long story."

"This person, or people, you're after...what's their game?" he asked.

Laura paused. Probably to evaluate what would be too much information. Honestly, Eri didn't know why they didn't just be quiet and let them go.

"Kidnapping and killing children," Laura said.

The man scratched his goatee with pursed lips. "That's not cool. And he's in my town. I think I know the cat."

"Really?" Laura crossed her arms.

"Yeah, we've had a few homeless kids go missing in the neighborhood." The man handed the bag to one of his goons and faced back to Laura. "Look, I don't know you, but I'm a good judge of character. I'm not okay with messing with kids. Capisce?"

"Agreed." Laura nodded. "And to be honest, we need some supplies to take them down. If you know how we could get some more guns and technology for a job, I think we could do some business."

Goatee reached in his jacket.

Eri raised her gun.

"I'm Antonio Dubois." He pulled out a card. "You call me. We'll see if we can help."

"I'm Laura." She took the card.

Eri lowered her gun and stepped back.

Laura shook his hand, and they passed by and down the steps.

The group visibly exhaled together.

"Okay, that was just crazy," Charlie said, entering and falling back onto one of the empty sleeping bags.

Eri walked in and closed the door behind them. "I'm glad you locked the door, Myers. That could have been bad."

"I'm glad you took the phone," Laura said. "We thought that was you, and we were about to open it without cover."

Eri folded to the ground with crossed legs. Normal almost felt normal for a few seconds.

"Well, something good may have come out if it." Laura lifted the card in the air. "We have made a friend."

"Why do you suppose he would help us?" Myers asked.

Bryce took the card and looked at it. "Because, he's into organized crime and knows two things: money and power. If we help him keep his territory intact, he'll help us."

Laura smiled with a nod. "Yep. Without a doubt. I could tell he probably works in guns and such."

"Do you think he believed us?" Myers asked. "About not being cops, I mean?"

"I think so. He gave me his card." Laura accepted the card back from Bryce and put it in her pocket.

"I wonder what was in the bag," Alicia said.

"Probably better we don't know." Myers set his gun on the kitchen counter. "If we did, then today probably would have ended differently."

"True." Charlie nodded.

"Now, let's air out our next play." Laura opened the blueprint again. "We have to get this done."

Charlie grabbed his laptop. "We need to get eyes in there."

"How can we get in there to do any recon?" Eri dropped down next to him. "Harding knows all of us."

"We need disguises," Laura said. "Who can take that on?"

All life drained from Myers's expression. As a con artist, Denise had been the queen of disguises. If anyone could have helped in this moment, it would have been her. Eri shot him a consoling glance.

"I've always said if we change genders, people are less likely to know you." Eri pulled her knees up and hugged them. "I think I should go in, but as a guy. Send pretty boy Bryce in as a girl."

Bryce's eyes bulged. "Um, you're joking."

Laura laughed. "She has a point. We can do that rather inexpensively without many supplies."

"Oh, brother." Bryce squeezed his eyes shut. "Are you sure Charlie isn't the better choice? He can hack into things while inside."

"I'm not as pretty, apparently." Charlie looked at Eri and winked.

She smiled. "Look, we aren't doing anything yet. We're just getting intel, right? So, we don't need Charlie now. And Bryce doesn't have a five o'clock shadow like the other guys. It will be more believable."

"I'm six foot two. You don't think that's a bit weird."

Eri hadn't thought of that.

"I'll go in as a boy, too," Laura offered.

Eri shook her head. "No, that won't work."

"Why not?"

Everyone looked at each other, no one answering.

"Why not?" Laura said again.

Bryce kissed the top of her head. "First, Harding really knows you. Second, you're not the most feminine girl."

"What's that supposed to mean?"

No one answered.

"Fine. I won't go. That means you, honey, are going to buck up and wear some heels and makeup."

Eri glanced at Charlie. Though he had stubble, it was blond. Maybe if he shaved. "You know, Charlie *is* only five six and already has long hair. If he shaved…"

Charlie glanced both ways. "Um…what?"

Laura nodded. "I agree."

"I second or third, I'll even fourth." Bryce raised his hand. "All those in favor?"

Everyone, minus Charlie, said, "Aye."

"It's settled then," Laura said. "We'll get supplies tonight and check it out in the morning."

****

Eri couldn't stop snickering. Her boyfriend looked

like a "girlfriend." *Ridiculous*. His dishwater blond hair was curled. He wore make up and a long dress. Though Laura tried to insist, he drew the line at nylons and opted for a pair of short boots instead.

"What are you laughing at?" Charlie grimaced.

"Have you looked in the mirror?" Eri smirked.

"Have you?" Charlie raised an eyebrow, nodding to the mirror behind them.

They cut some of her hair and adhered a tiny mustache to her lip. With mascara, they gave her a fade on the chin to give the appearance of shadow. Her hair was pulled back in a ponytail worn by many of her male cousins, and she wore black frames complemented by a man's suit and tie. With a little lipstick, she could easily be in a 1980's Robert Palmer music video.

"Come on, dear," Eri said in a mock deep voice.

Myers, dressed as a limo driver, came around and let them out. He had been instructed to wear shades, keep his head down, and quickly return to the vehicle.

Eri stepped out first and offered her hand to Charlie. Then she looped her arm and Charlie grabbed her bicep. They gave each other one last glance, took a deep breath in unison, and started for the entrance of a building only a few blocks from the Capitol. A doorman opened the outer door, and Eri opened the second, letting Charlie walk in first. She was trying hard to be a gentleman, but it was taking everything in her to not break down laughing. This entire thing was ludicrous.

Together, they walked through the lobby. Eri busied herself with a flyer on a kiosk, watching the receptionist. It was important to determine if they stop or stay confident and keep going? Sometimes confidence could make people ignore something they shouldn't. Another couple walked into the elevator. The woman seemed preoccupied on the phone. Eri nodded to Charlie. He nodded back.

Together, they strutted to the elevator, heads high, like they belonged there. Charlie pushed the button with his painted finger. Eri glanced at the sign listing floors. Maybe Laura should have done this. She would know their shell company instantly.

"Which one?" Eri whispered.

"That one." Charlie pointed to Cyber Talent Agency. "That name was inside the files."

The door slid open, and they stepped in, holding their gaze on the floor to avoid any cameras. Charlie hit twelve. It raised about two floors, and the door slid open. This was not the floor they chose. The couple exchanged glances. An armed security guard stood only feet from them.

"Sorry, wrong floor." Charlie giggled in his best girl voice.

The door closed, and Charlie tried to hit the twelfth floor again. The door opened again. He hit lobby. Charlie pulled something from his pocket and slipped it under the handrail in the elevator, just before it opened, and they stepped out. This time they didn't meander. Eri prayed they weren't compromised.

They hurried through the lobby, half expecting a bullet in the back. Finally on the street, Myers came around and let them in.

Within minutes, they were back in the apartment; her heart still beating wildly. A flash of Denise dropping by a single bullet hole increased her fear. She couldn't have another incident like before.

Alicia stared out the window.

"Stay away from any windows," Eri snapped.

Alicia backed off.

"Did something go wrong?" Laura asked with concern in her voice.

Eri shook her head. The group circled up. "We punched the twelfth floor, but it opened on second with an armed guard. We couldn't get farther than that."

"My assumption is that the receptionist is a decoy. The real gatekeeper is on the second floor. No matter what floor you hit, it will open on two." Charlie started his laptop. "But it wasn't a total bust. I inserted a miniature bug camera. Next time someone enters the elevator; it will exit floor two and offer full disclosure of the place."

"So, are you saying that no matter what floor you push, it is going to open on floor two?" Laura asked. "Can you explain how the bug works?"

"It's a tiny drone." Charlie pinched his fingers together and opened them about an inch. "Cool technology from our new friends."

Laura crossed her arms and paced among the makeshift beds on the floor. "At least we know they are there. I hope your bug can find out how many men there are. Then we can start to plan." She leaned against the kitchenette, facing them. Her mind obviously deep in thought.

From what Eri knew of her, Laura lived for this kind of puzzle. Years in the agency must have warped her sense of adventure. Though she'd never admit it, Eri enjoyed the danger to some extent herself. It made her feel alive.

"I've arranged to meet Antonio for some tech

supplies, and we'll go from there," Laura said.

Bryce joined her with arms crossed. "When are we meeting him?"

"We're not. *I am*." Laura flipped around to face the counter. "Alone."

Bryce turned with her. Though they tried to be quiet, Eri had great hearing. "You can't be serious?" he said. "I'm not letting you go alone."

"You don't have a choice. Either I go, or we don't have them."

Bryce slid his hand onto her wrist. "At least have some back up."

"If he smells anyone else, he'll be gone." She kissed his cheek. "You know I'm good. Nothing to worry about. I've got this."

Chapter Twenty-Five

Laura stepped out in the dark alley and tucked Antonio's card back in her jacket pocket. A can rattled a few feet away. Her hand touched the gun in her waistband, preparing herself for whatever might be lurking in the shadows. Everyone knew she was good, but this was maybe even more than she could handle. Why did she come down here alone? Sure Antonio told her to, but when had she ever listened to a "bad" guy.

Headlights entered the alleyway. She faced the long, brown sedan, squinting. It drove a few feet from her and stopped. The lights remained on as three of the doors opened. Antonio stepped out, along with two gunmen adorned in gang tattoos. Her pulse quickened—every sense alert, ready.

"Laura." Antonio smirked.

"Antonio." She feigned a smile. "Thanks for meeting me."

"I have your supplies…" He rubbed his hands together and then brought his two fingers to his chin. "But I wonder what you might do for me."

Nerves threatened to judder her body. Long ago, she had learned how to steady her core. It took hours in a frozen fridge to learn how, but she mastered it. Tapping into that learned behavior, she regained control. "As I explained earlier, I don't have much money, and you said you had another idea." With confidence, she stepped toward him. "I'm listening."

He walked around her, rubbing his goatee. "The FBI has a video file that could harm someone I care about. I need it to disappear."

"Explain."

"You will need to break into the FBI, download it, and erase it on their end."

Her heart sank. Break into the FBI? That was crazy. But what other choice did they have? Her team was broke. Desperate. They needed this exchange. Without it, they might as well hide, not fight. "Okay. Can we do it after we're done?"

"Assuming you understand the ramifications of trying to skip out on our deal?"

"Of course."

Antonio snapped and one of the gunmen reached in back of the car and withdrew two black military duffle bags. "The details are inside, along with your supplies." He handed her the bags and then moved to the car door. "We'll be in touch."

Laura didn't speak. She didn't have to. The deal was made. Their fate set.

The car rolled back and out of sight.

Though cold, her hands were sweaty. She put a bag on her back like a backpack and worked to grip the second bag as she started back for the tenement. Now the harder part—telling her crew. Worse. Telling Bryce. He'd kill her.

She ran several blocks before the weight of the bags overcame her, and she hailed a taxi. They took her within feet of the tenement door. She paid and stepped out, ready for her fate. Inside, the thumping of base could be heard. A few junkies lay at the base of the steps. She stepped over them and started up the stairs. Laughter could be heard from inside. That would soon end. She wrapped on the door. A few seconds and Myers leaned out. He opened the door and let her inside.

"How'd it go?" he asked.

"Well, we got the supplies." She tossed the bag on the counter. Eri unzipped it and Charlie glanced inside.

"I hear a 'but' in there somewhere," Bryce said, walking to her.

"Yeah, maybe."

"What is the deal?" Bryce asked.

Please don't get mad. Please don't get mad. "We have to steal something for them, too."

"From S.I.U.?" Myers asked.

Laura chewed on her lip. Her heart hammered in her chest, her pulse audible in her ears. "Not exactly."

Bryce and Myers both stood on each side of her, arms crossed, daring her to continue.

"From the F.B.I."

"What?!?" Bryce backed up, shaking his head. "Are you nuts?"

Laura knew they'd be upset, but she didn't expect this. Myers started throwing a fit, cursing and hitting things. *Okay, that is kind of normal.* Charlie began pacing, frantically wiping the makeup off on an old T-shirt, mumbling to himself. Eri just stared at her, unmoving, almost making it more disturbing. The two girls chattered nervously behind them.

"Are you nuts?" Bryce asked again.

Maybe a little. But what Antonio wanted would be easy for their team. It was a simple download and delete of a file. Nothing too taxing. "I'm sorry. We are almost out of money and have nothing to trade other than our skills."

Myers kicked the wall, and his foot went through.

"Chill, dude," Charlie said and then looked at Laura. "What do we need for that?"

"Just you downloading and deleting a file. I don't think it will be hard. Not for you." She offered a closed mouth smile.

Charlie rolled his eyes.

"Just life in prison. I've been there." Myers punched his fist in his hand, before expelling a new string of expletives. "No desire to go back."

Helena touched Myers's arm. For some reason, he seemed to settle a bit.

Bryce walked to her side and held her hand. "I know you are just trying to do what you can with what we have."

"I am."

"But consider all of us. You didn't include us on this decision." The hurt in his eyes tugged at her heart. He was right. She was wrong. *Now what?*

"I'm sorry. You're right." She looked from him to the group. "I didn't know what else to do. He said come alone. So I did. I had to make the choice then and there. But you're right. I should have been more forthcoming."

Bryce kissed her forehead. Charlie nodded and folded to the ground with his laptop. Myers stopped pacing and leaned against the wall.

"Look, we don't have to do it until our fight is over. We'll figure it out later." Laura dropped hearing devices, silencers, and a wad of cash on the counter. "In the meantime, we're in business."

****

Laura stared at Helena. An idea was circulating in her mind, and it was crazy. But then so was their life. They stopped being rational a year ago.

Helena glanced up from a book of poetry Eri had loaned her and titled her head sideways. "Is everything okay?"

"I have an idea."

Everyone stopped what he or she was doing and pushed in.

Laura stepped in front of them, afraid to say it for the response she would get. She had to lay this out carefully. "The problem we have is that guard is the only one who can get us to the other floors, right?"

Charlie nodded.

"So, he is basically the key. We need to unlock him."

The team stared at her, obviously not following.

"Look, don't bite my head off, especially you, Myers…" She glanced at him, already starting to pace. "But we need someone who is not on their watch list to get to him. If we trained Helena—"

"No way, Black," Myers snapped.

"Myers, hear me out." She cut him off, then softly said, "Please."

He glared at her, but motioned for her to continue.

"It is a simple solution. We all tail him and find out where he hangs out after hours. Then we send Helena, dressed to the hilt, into the bar to roofie him." Lara held up her hands in order to continue. "We bring him back here and find out what we can."

"Roofie?" Alicia asked.

"Drug him with Rohypnol," Laura said. "Our new

186

friend could probably help us get some, along with some other supplies I'll need."

"Why Helena?" Myers asked.

"Because, I guarantee our faces are on some wanted list in their lunchroom. I'm positive he would spot us the second we entered the bar."

"She's right," Eri said. "Helena is known by Harding, but probably not by some watch dog. Harding might not even know she is with us."

"It's the lowest danger. She just has to spike his drink. You guys will take it from there. And Eri, you would stay dressed in your male alter ego a few feet back." Laura peered over at Helena. Surprisingly, she didn't seem scared. "What do you think?"

Helena shrugged. "Yeah, I'll do it."

"Your male alter ego needs a name," Charlie teased.

Eri laughed. "I've already named him."

"What?"

"You'll know soon enough."

"He needs a name so we can call him," Charlie replied.

Eri winked, then looked at Laura. "So, what first?"

"I'll train Helena, and the rest of you..." Laura glanced at Myers. "Start tailing him."

Chapter Twenty-Six

Eri entered the dark bar. It took a moment for her eyes to adjust. The walls were black, filled with florescent beer logo signs and loud rock music. A mirror behind the bar showed her the room. She quickly found a seat in the back corner. Their mark was already nursing a drink at the bar.

A second later, Helena sauntered in. Her long black hair lay in folds around her bare shoulders. She wore a short red cocktail dress to go with the three-inch heels Eri bought off a hooker in their building. The girl was gorgeous. No wonder Myers was so protective. Eri smiled.

Helena saddled up to the bar and ordered a club soda. Laura had told her to avoid an ID check. She may be twenty-three, but she looked like a kid. The bartender grabbed a glass, shot some clear liquid in it, placed it on the counter, and hit it with a lime slice.

Now it was time for Laura's plan. Helena nursed her drink, waiting to see if the man would say something first. Laura had said the better tactics always come when it is the mark's idea. But not all men were looking for love, so a plan "B" was already in place. When he didn't look at Helena, she turned to him and asked him for the time.

The man pushed his sleeve back, glanced at a watch, and said something.

Helena nodded and then started sniffling. Laura taught her to keep it simple, not dramatic. Too crazy and he was likely to move away from her.

"It looks to me like you need a stiffer drink," the man said.

She dabbed her eyes with the drink napkin before responding. "I'm only twenty, so I knew he wouldn't serve me."

The man smiled. "I can help with that." He lifted a finger.

The bartender walked over. "Yeah, Joey, what you need?"

"My friend needs a shot."

The man looked at her and back to Joey. He nodded, poured amber liquid into a shot glass, and passed it back. *Uh oh.* Had Helena ever drank before? If not, she may be too drunk to deliver.

"Thanks." Helena held her shot up to toast him.

The man mirrored her.

Helena shot the liquid to her throat without a flinch.

Eri ran a hand over her head and silently prayed in Mandarin. *Please do not let her fail.*

Helena slid away from the bar and started for the door. She winked at Eri as she passed by and out of the place.

Eri focused back on Joey. Somehow, Helena had slipped him the pill, but she wasn't sure when. Within seconds, he began to sway. He slid out and started for the restroom. Myers and Bryce followed him in. Eri stood and walked out the front entrance. They would meet her at home with the cargo.

The sidewalks were slippery, and the air bitter.

Christmas decorations and Santas were beginning to pop up around the businesses. Would this be over before Christmas? She hoped so. It would be nice to actually enjoy the holiday and not be running for their lives. She reached the apartment, sprinted up the stairs, and produced their coded knock on the outside door.

Laura opened it with gun behind her back.

"It's me." Eri passed her and smiled at Helena. "Slick on slipping it. I didn't even see you do it."

"I did it when he ordered my drink." Her smiled indicated the joy of her accomplishment.

They waited about ten minutes, and the secret knock sounded again. Laura and Eri readied their guns, but lowered them at their side. They let them in with the almost unconscious Joey drooping between their two shoulders. They deposited him on a metal chair they found in one of the other abandoned rooms and secured him with duct tape.

Eri, Charlie, and Laura stayed behind him, not wanting their faces in his memory in any way. Myers and Bryce put on ski masks. They stood straight, with arms crossed in front, like armed guards. Helena sauntered in front of him.

"Wake him up," Laura said.

Myers placed a vial of ammonia under his nose.

The man shook his head side to side, and his eyes slowly opened.

"Are you okay? It looks like you had too much to drink," Helena said smooth as butter.

His wrists struggled to free themselves.

Laura shot a syringe of truth serum into his neck and mouthed with a hand raised, "Five minutes."

"In a few minutes, I'm going to ask you some

questions, and you're going to be honest with me."

He began to curse her in another language Eri didn't know.

Helena put a finger to his mouth. "Ah, ah, ah. No need for name calling."

Eri and Laura exchanged amused glances. This girl had more skill than they knew.

"Now, I need you to tell me about your job."

The man wobbled in the chair, trying to break his bindings.

"Joey, you're not going anywhere. You're surrounded by my people, all armed, very dangerous, I assure you." Her thick accent made this all the more comical. "You're tied to a chair, and you're on some serious drugs." She patted his face with patronization implied. "So, you might as well chill down and talk to me."

"I will…kill…you…" Joey spat out.

She raised her eyebrows. "Ah, Joey, don't start with the mean words, just when I thought we had an understanding. I will have to make you suffer." She nodded at Myers.

Myers stepped to him and punched him hard enough that the man fell back in the chair. Bryce pushed him back up.

"Now, my good friend, you have something in your blood stream that should have taken affect by now. I'm going to ask you some questions, and I expect you to answer them truthfully." She circled him and winked at the three behind him. Charlie gave her a thumbs up, Laura nodded, and even Eri couldn't have been more proud.

This girl was a natural. It almost scared her. The

possibility of her being a mole suddenly seemed possible. "If you don't answer me truthfully, then I will sic my hooded friends on you. They are hoping that happens. Both are bloodthirsty and would love nothing more than a chance to hurt you. Are you ready to answer my questions?"

The man's eyes were wide, his lip trembling. Fear was now present. He nodded.

"Whom do you work for?" she asked.

"A talent agency."

Helena placed her hands on the back of both of his shoulders and squeezed. "That's the answer you give others who don't know who you are. I want to know what you would say if Agent Harding asked you."

His eyes widened on the name. *Bingo.*

"Now let's try again. Whom do you work for?"

The grimace on his face indicated his fight against the serum, but Laura had given him a strong dose. No one could muster that much will power. "S.I.U."

The group exchanged looks around the room. *Confirmation.*

"Yes, we know this. Tell me, what floor is Agent Harding located on?"

Joey closed his eyes and grunted out the words, "The basement."

Helena glanced at Laura.

Laura motioned her over and whispered in her ear. Helena nodded and leaned down to his face with a pout. "A twelve story building, why would Harding be in a basement?"

"For protection. He's the top dog." Giggling, Joey sounded wasted now. The serum was at its max capacity. They had to work fast.

Helena smiled. "You're doing great, Joey. Now, tell me who is on floors three through twelve?"

"They're prisons, dorms, and training facilities."

Prisons? Like the one they had endured in the jungle? Eri motioned Helena over. "Ask him why they chose this location?"

"Why is S.I.U. here? Why put this in the middle of the city? Isn't it risky?"

Joey swayed his head back-and-forth, obviously high. "Nah, man. It's brilliant. We're right here, we the people, government, agencies…many of who work for us. It's so close, no one can see it—dig it."

Helena peered back to Laura.

Laura mouthed, "How do we get to the other floors?"

"How do we get to the other floors?" Helena said.

Joey laughed. "You don't. Only I do."

Laura rolled her eyes. She spun her finger in a circular motion, indicating Helena should keep going.

"What do you mean by that, Joey?"

"That it is bio-protected. Only me and Carlos can get you into that building."

"When is it protected?"

"24/7. Except…"

"Except?"

He grimaced.

"Except?"

"Except when the building is empty."

"When is the building empty?"

He leaned his head back and yawned.

Helena slapped his cheek a couple of times. "Joey, stay with me. When is it empty?"

"When everyone is in the field, but that happens

193

never. Ever. Never. Ever."

"When does it happen next?" Helena asked.

"Maybe Monday. Big ta-do at the White House. Maybe then." He blew through his lips. "But who knows. Nobody knows, said the snow man."

Charlie covered his mouth, obviously trying not to laugh. Eri shot him a warning look. His hand dropped.

Laura pointed to her hand, eye, and then pretended to pull blood from her arm.

"How is it bio-protected? Do you have to give them blood?" Helena asked.

"DNA scan, duh. Eye, hand, and once a day—blood." A silly smile adhered to his face. He was gone. Pretty soon he would be too gone to answer. He closed his eyes and started to snore.

Helena slapped his face to wake him up. "So, if I had your eyeball, your finger, and a drop of your blood, I could get in."

"Yep." He smiled, eyes still closed.

Helena walked around and whispered in Laura's ear. "How do we get all that?"

Laura smiled. "We were able to get what we needed from Antonio." From behind, she covered Joey's eyes with a rag, then grabbed a vial, and drew his blood. She then had the masked men open his eye, as Charlie scanned it. They ended with taking his fingerprints.

Laura nodded to Myers and Bryce. "Take him. Make sure you give him the other shot."

Helena passed them his wallet and keys. "The address is inside."

Myers and Bryce carried him out of the room.

"What is the other shot?" Alicia asked.

"A sleeping agent. It will make him think he just fell asleep and all of this was just a very bad dream."

"Myers slapped him though," Helena said.

"Can be explained by a bar fight." Laura reached for Helena. "You were so good! I only had a few hours to train you, and you acted like you have been doing this for years. Welcome officially to the team!"

Helena hugged her and peeked at Eri.

Eri nodded with a grin. "You did well."

"Thank you. I actually enjoyed myself," Helena said.

The women laughed. "We could tell."

Charlie sat on the floor and opened his laptop.

Eri saddled next to him. "So, Obi Won, what now?"

"First of all, a *Star Wars* reference is very sexy and will get you pretty much anywhere. Second, we have to find a way to achieve all three bio scans in the field." He began clicking into different programs.

"Are we sure we want to put Joey back? Couldn't he help us if this all doesn't work out?"

"He said they might be off Monday. Risky, but it may be our only shot." Laura began scribbling on a black notepad. Her mind was always going. Eri had learned to just leave her alone when she processed.

It seemed like an hour, but finally, the secret knock sounded at the door. Helena opened it, and both men hugged her.

"You were so good," Myers said.

She blushed.

"So, he is all snug in bed?" Eri asked.

Laura looked up. "I hope not. Did you do what I asked?"

Bryce nodded. "Yeah, we placed him face down, feet half on, half off the bed with an empty bottle of booze on the floor. Lipstick on the shirt. And a woman's thong under the sheets. And no money or credit cards in his wallet."

Eri had to laugh. Only Laura would think of that.

"What does all that mean?" Alicia asked.

Helena smiled. "They are making it look like he had a hot date who screwed him."

"It is more likely he'll believe that, than the crazy dream we gave him." Laura sat in the empty chair and sighed. "All right, friends, let's order pizza, and get this done."

Chapter Twenty-Seven

Laura started her stopwatch. They had exactly twenty-three minutes. The lobby was empty, only a soft glow from a security light. Bryce kept a close distance to Laura just outside.

"Eri is positioned to enter from one of the windows above," Charlie said through the com link. "The cameras are looped; you're free to move."

Laura and Bryce bolted across the lobby. The clump of their boots was anything but stealth. The elevator opened. The doors slid closed, and they ascended to the next floor automatically. Laura and Bryce readied their weapons. No going back now. The door opened. No one. *Too easy.* She plugged the bio scans to the various components on the wall, hit the B on the elevator panel, and waited quietly for the doors to close once again.

"Are you sure we want Harding first?" Bryce whispered.

"Eri is going after the prisoners. This is our best move."

He nodded.

The pace of their decent made Laura anxious. Her neck tensed. They only needed to travel down two floors, but the length of ride felt like twenty. When it finally opened, a large man stood there, arms crossed and a scowl on his face.

Without hesitation, Laura slammed the butt of the gun toward his face. The man parried and counter jabbed. Laura stumbled back.

Bryce's fist cracked against the man's jaw, pushing the guy into Laura's round kick. The man fell, but was still moving. She netted another punch into his temple. His body relaxed. They lugged the man around a corner, shoved him into a small server room, and then crept back into the hallway. The vast gray, cemented passage echoed and only a few fluorescent lights, every twenty feet or so, lit their way. Laura increased their pace, not sure when the corridor would end. Finally, there was a double entrance with a glass slit at the top. She peered through it. The interior was indistinguishable.

"Silencers on," Laura whispered.

She fastened hers, then inched one of the doors open with her foot, and slinked in. The room appeared empty except for chains, meat hooks, and other torturing devices. A pungent smell of rotting flesh permeated the air. She winced and worked to breathe through her mouth. A chill swept through her. Something wasn't right. A lock clicked behind them.

They exchanged glances and knew. Both rushed to the entrance. The handle wouldn't turn. Bryce kicked at it. Laura used her hip. Over and over, they tried, but it wouldn't open. A slip of paper slid underneath the crack at the bottom.

So glad you could join us. Sleep tight. Joe.

A compressed hiss pierced the silence. She fired at the window. Bullet proof. Smoke began to billow into the room. Panic was apparent in Bryce's gaze, mirroring her own. A trap. They had failed. This was it.

She grabbed him and squeezed tight. Her eyes grew heavy. All senses left her. No longer could she feel Bryce's arms. Her body wilted, numb. Unable to stand, she slumped to the ground. Bryce fell to her side. Darkness.

****

When she opened her eyes, Laura was chained to the wall. Bryce lay asleep on the floor a few inches away. The door opened, and Joe came in. "Awe, you're awake. Wonderful." He walked to a table that was decorated with vicious tools and needles and picked up a syringe. "I felt so welcome and had so much fun at your house the other day that I decided to share the same courtesy."

He pushed the syringe into her arm. It burned. Almost immediately, her mind floated. "What you failed to realize is that we train for such kidnappings. I could have held off, but I figured, if I knew when you'd come, then I'd have the upper hand."

Her tongue lay heavy in her mouth. "Monday?" she slurred.

"Brilliant, no?" His tone full of personal satisfaction. "And the basement. Do you really think Agent Harding would be down here? He's the boss. Bosses don't hang out in scary dungeons."

The room whirled in dull color. She squeezed her eyes closed, then open, but couldn't focus. How could Bryce and she possibly get out of this one? Her only hope was the rest of the team. Hopefully, they were safe and coming to get them.

"I will let that take effect and be back in a bit. Enjoy your trip, my dear. And if you think you're trained for this drug, you'd be wrong. It's my own personal cocktail." He whistled as he sauntered out, pride radiating from him.

Bryce peeked through his eyelids and smiled. "I thought he'd never leave." He slid from the wall and showed his freed hands. "Come on, let me get you out. They aren't tight enough, so if you…" It clicked and fell. "And you're free."

His arm slid under hers. "Can you walk?"

She shook her head.

He lifted her into his arms and moved to the exit. Surprisingly, the door was unlocked. Joe was not as smart as he thought. *Never be sloppy or assuming when dealing with an agent. Rule number one.* Laura attempted to grin, but the muscles in her face would not contract.

Bryce tiptoed down the corridor, trying hard not to make any sound in the echoing space. The elevator was just feet away. It opened. Laura's heart stopped. Joe stood inside the elevator space. He flicked through several papers and then looked up to see Laura and Bryce. His mouth gaped and eyes froze.

Bryce set Laura down.

Joe dropped his file and swung.

Bryce ducked. Fist. Swing. Duck. Maneuver. Kick. Dizzy, Laura could barely keep track of who was who and what was happening. A gun fired. Laura panicked. She fought to discern who survived, amidst her blurry vision. The smell of gun oil, and then a body dropped.

"Ready?" Bryce said through the fog.

Relief. With all the strength she could muster, she swung her arms around him and squeezed. Tears welled in her eyes, against her nature. He picked her up again and carried her into the elevator.

Her tongue adhered like stone in her mouth, but she worked to say, "Pris-o-ners."

"You can't help. I will get you to safety and take Myers."

She nodded.

Outside, the cool brisk air burned her face. Myers opened the door to the limo, and Bryce laid her inside.

"What happened?" Myers asked.

"We were compromised. She's been pumped full of something, and Joe is dead." Bryce kissed her lips. She could only feel the pressure, not the soft sweetness that made her usually smile. "Sleep, my dear. We'll take care of it."

Laura closed her eyes.

"Myers, are you okay to come back in with me?" Bryce asked.

"You bet."

The door banged closed, and Laura drifted off to sleep.

Chapter Twenty-Eight

Eri scaled the building beyond the twelfth floor to the roof. The top was covered in gravel and air ducts. She quickly found her way to the main ventilation shaft and removed the cover. She spoke through her ear piece, "Okay, Charlie. Turn off the air."

"Done."

The buzzing of the fan ceased as the blades stopped spinning. Using several tools from her belt, she removed the outer fan and then lifted it onto the roof. A ten-foot drop separated her from the base of the vent. Keeping her hands and feet pressed against the metallic walls, she shifted herself to the bottom. She sat crouched as she paced down the ventilation halls. "Now where, Charlie?"

"To your left about two yards, you'll see the grate, then… Wait…stop!"

She froze. "What?"

"Do you see any dust?"

She laughed. "Yeah, I'm sitting in dust bunnies."

"Blow some of it in front of you."

She scooped up a handful and blew. Refractions of light shimmered from the dust. "Infrared lasers? Now what?"

"One second." A rapid succession of tapping riddled the com, followed by the obnoxious sound of Charlie sipping from an aluminum can. The space filled with moisture. Like a microwave, heat began to swelter Eri. Sweat dripped into her eyes, burning. She wiped her face with her sleeve. A sharp tingle overwhelmed her feet; she shifted herself to compensate the nagging pain. "Hurry, Charlie. This is getting very uncomfortable."

"One second."

"You said that one-hundred and twenty seconds ago."

"There!" A slap against wood, possibly his desk, crackled against the earpiece. "More dust, sweetheart."

She grimaced. "Now, that's where I draw the line."

"To more dust?"

"To sweetheart."

He chuckled. "You know it's enduring?"

She blew. Nothing. She tried again. No refraction. "I think I'm good." She breathed in steadily. "Promise me I'm good."

"I'm ninety-nine point one percent sure you're good to go."

"Should I be afraid of that point nine percent?" One foot inched forward, followed by the other. The lasers appeared gone. Within seconds, she found herself at the vent. Pressure filled her lungs as she remembered to breathe. The room below her was dark and silent. A single office desk was positioned below her. She unscrewed the grate and placed it to the side, then lowered herself until she could drop to the desk. Metal cabinets lined the walls of the enclosed office. She slid down to the tiled surface and unlocked the door that stood opposite of her. Cracking it open, she peered in both directions. No movement was visible, but several sounds came from down the corridor.

She slithered into the hallway, low against the floor as she moved toward the noise. The lights in the room ahead shined light into the dark space. Two agents, one male and one female, chatted by the side of a computer monitor, dressed in the traditional black trainee uniforms. Eri fumbled through her pockets and grasped a single dime. Tossing it, the light danced across it as it rebounded off a window on the other side of the room.

The agents both turned toward the sound. Eri dashed toward them and round-kicked the man in the face, while her hand struck the female's neck. The male landed hard against the wall and dropped unconscious. Staggering, the female raised her hands defensively. Eri jammed her fist into the woman's side. The agent forced Eri back with a flourish of punches, but it was obvious she was still green.

Eri ducked back and flipped herself in the air, hitting the wall with her foot; she sprung forward and grappled the enemy to the ground. The agent clawed the air as Eri looped her arms around the woman's neck and legs to paralyze her. Trapped, the agent became motionless against Eri's grasp. Only a faint breathe stirred from the incapacitated woman.

The room fell still. Eri slipped the cap and outer vest from the agent's body and then ripped a badge from the female's shirt. The vest fit loosely, but otherwise functional. Eri put the cap on and hurried back down the hall. On one wall, a stenciled sign read "Barracks" with an arrow pointing to the left. Another said "Lock up," pointing to the right. She ran toward the lock up. A guard stood at the end. Eri slowed her pace and stilled her breath.

"Good evening," she said.

"You're not supposed to be here," he responded sternly.

The memory of so many movies brought to mind the phrase, "Where's the bathroom?" But that would hardly work. She held back her smile. "I was told by Harding to come relieve you."

He raised an eyebrow. "I haven't been told that?"

Eri shrugged and started to back up. "No skin off my nose. I'd rather be hanging with the group that just got back."

He stared at her a moment. "Wait, let me call it in first."

Now what?

"Tell him to go ahead," Charlie said in her ear. "I'll intercept."

"Yeah, call it in."

"Level twelve, guard station to main station. Come in."

"Main station, over," Charlie said.

"Confirm that Agent…" he glanced at the badge on the vest. "Riley is to relieve me at this hour."

"Affirmative. Agent Riley is to relieve Station Twelve at 2100. It appears she is late."

"Yes, sir, it appears she is. Shall I reprimand her?" His gaze traveled over her body, and Eri cringed.

"No, we will discuss it with her later. Please resign your post. Main Station out."

Charlie, I could kiss you. Eri forced back the smile.

"So, you check out." He handed her a wad of keys. "Do not go in there. We have strict orders to stay out. Understood?"

Eri nodded. "So then what is the wad of keys for?"

"In case something happens or if any senior

officers are up here and need a key." He sat his baton on small desk and then handed her a white index card. "This is the code for the alarm. Only use it if you are ordered to."

"I assume that is before opening the doors."

She smiled like she was joking.

The guard stared at her, not amused. "Are you sure you're up to this?"

"Absolutely. I've been asked a few times, and this is the first time it fit my work schedule."

"Be careful not to overdo it," Charlie said in her ear.

"I hope you have a good rest of your night." Eri attached the keys to her belt, pushed the baton in her loop, and the paper into her front pant pocket. "No worries here."

"I'll be back at 0900."

She nodded.

He gave her one final glance and then sauntered down the hall.

Eri exhaled. Her head spun from the adrenaline filtering through her blood stream.

"You were so good," Charlie said.

"You can congratulate me later."

"Oh, I intend to," Charlie said with meaning.

Eri shook her head and smiled. She pulled the paper from her pocket and stared at it. A computer digital number had been taped to the card: AT4MN9L2. "Okay, here is the code. Ready?"

"Go."

"Alpha Tango Four Mike November Niner Lima Two."

He repeated it back as the keyboard clicked

through the earpiece. "Here goes nothing."

"Nothing like making a girl's heart skip."

"All the girls say that."

"What girls?"

Charlie chuckled. "Okay, try the first key."

Eri fumbled with the ring and tried several before one opened the outer gate door. It slid to the side, echoing down the hall. She prayed no one heard it. Each side of the lock up hallway held thick metal doors with small slits. She came to the first one on the left and peeked inside. A young girl lay crumpled on the floor.

Eri unlocked and slid it open, revealing more bar doors. *Great.* She fumbled with more keys until locating the appropriate one. She released it, stepping inside.

Cowering, a girl slowly peered up through tangles of red hair. Her face and arms were bruised and dry blood stuck to her nose. She wore dirty tan pajamas, almost as if they had originally pulled her from bed. She couldn't have been more than fourteen.

"I'm Eri. What's your name?"

Barely audible, she whispered, "Willow."

"Come on, Willow, we have to get you out of here." Eri bent down to help her up, then touched her earpiece to keep it from falling out. "Charlie, I'm going to need a lot more help here."

"Laura is out of commission, but Bryce and Myers are in the building. You want them on the twelfth floor?"

"Yeah, left of the elevator."

"I'll see what I can do. You'll be off coms for a second."

She nodded as if he could see her. Reaching down,

Eri lifted the young girl and helped her just outside the door. "Go ahead and sit here. I need to check the other cells."

"They'll kill me if they see me."

Eri rubbed her shoulder. "There are others on the way. Just sit tight. They'll be here shortly." She worked to unlock the second door. It took three keys, but it finally opened. A boy charged her like an animal. Eri flipped around and dropped kicked him to the ground, landing her foot at his throat. "I am here to help you, but if you do that again, I will lock you back in and throw away the key. You understand?"

The young boy attempted to nod under her foot.

"Can I remove my foot without being attacked?"

He nodded again.

She stepped off, staring at him.

He pushed back to a sitting position. The boy had the whitest blond hair she had ever seen on a young person. It stuck up like he had been electrocuted. Contrasting to that were his dark eyebrows, long eyelashes, and steel-blue eyes. Though he was thin, he had broad shoulders and stood almost six foot. She gaged him about sixteen. "I've been planning my escape for months."

"Well, that wasn't going to work." She put a hand out to him and lifted him to his feet. His frame was longer than his weight. Had they been starving him? "Why are you guys in here?"

"We all messed up one way or another. We're waiting either reconditioning or, for most, extermination."

Eri's heart sank. Extermination. Like they were insects, not viable human beings with souls. "Sit outside here. I want to get the rest."

The boy slid to the ground and glanced at the red head to his left. "Hi, Willow."

Willow offered a closed mouth smile, but said nothing.

He glanced back at Eri, while she fiddled with more keys. "I'm Theodore, though my friends call me Teddy. You rescued me, so Teddy it is to you."

"Teddy likes to talk," Willow whispered.

Eri smiled. Her hands would be full with this bunch. He probably got in trouble for prattling on. Not once did he stop talking, as she continued to unlock doors and bring kid after kid out. The oldest was maybe seventeen; the youngest looked eight. Memories of her own capture were still fresh. Seeing this broke her heart. S.I.U. was not destroyed; it was only asleep.

Why did they think arresting Greenstone would finish this evil? Was this giant impossible to destroy? No way could she believe that. There was too much pain attached, too many shattered lives. They had to believe they could win. That somehow they could save more children from the same fate of becoming murderers, or worse, the fate Denise encumbered. Whatever it took, she was in the game until they were all destroyed. That was way more important than a "normal life" with her boyfriend.

She touched her earpiece. "Charlie, this is my life until it's over, understand?"

There was a long pause before he responded, "Me too."

Eri glanced back at the lot of them, wiping tears from her cheeks. Dirty, hurt, forlorn—children shouldn't be treated this way. Humans shouldn't be treated this way. It was almost too much.

"Myers and Bryce should be to your location in less than a minute," Charlie said in her ear. "They had a few distractions on the elevator, but it sounds like the problems are neutralized."

Eri sighed with reprieve. There were a total of eighteen prisoners. Getting them out of here would be tricky. Though they may be agents, all of them appeared worse for wear. Thin frames, bruised skin, dried blood, and some barely alive.

"Did they feed you and give you water?" Eri asked Teddy.

Teddy pursed his lips and sighed. "Water about every other day. Food maybe twice a week."

No water or water for that long could take any life. It was like a test of wills. "Come on, let's see about getting you all out of here. Who is strong enough to help others?"

Teddy raised his hand, along with a few other guys. Most of the girls appeared frail and weak. Eri wasn't sure they could make it. Luckily, the "Calvary" arrived in the form of Myers and Bryce.

"So, we have eighteen kids. Only three of the guys think they can help." Eri took the canteen off of Myers belt and passed it to Teddy. "Drink and pass." As he complied, she continued, "We need to figure this out quickly. Any threats we should know about?"

"No, it seems pretty clear, but we can't go out the front." Myers said. "Too many agents down there now to get eighteen kids passed them. How did you get in here?"

Eri shook her head. That was hard, even for her. "I don't think they could get up that pipe and through the ducts. There were some long drops." She touched her earpiece. "Suggestions, my prince?"

"There is a service elevator that only goes to the second floor, but maybe if you took them all down that way and then down the stairwell."

Eri glanced at Myers and Bryce.

"Yeah, let's do it," Bryce said. "It seems like our only option."

"Where is the elevator," Eri asked Charlie.

"Go back toward where you dropped in. It is just past that room. I don't see any heat signatures right now, so you should be okay."

Eri grabbed Willow. Teddy helped another small girl. Myers balanced two, as did Bryce. A few of the older guys took a few younger girls, and the older girls worked to go it on their own.

They plodded down hall at a tortoise pace. Eri kept shushing them. Finally, the elevator was in sight. *Oh no*. A keypad lay on the side of the metal door. "Charlie, we need a code."

"Try the one on the index card."

She had forgotten it. *Yes, of course. Alpha Tango Four Mike November Niner Lima Two.* After the last number, it beeped and then began to open. Everyone piled into a tight squeeze. Eri hugged everyone tight, determined to all go down together. Myers and Bryce stood at the front, guns ready.

The elevator crept to the bottom floor. As the door slid open, an agent reached for his gun. *Pop, pop.* Myers sent the agent to the ground. The group shifted out around the body and toward the stairwell. Bryce went first, and Myers covered from the rear. It took forever, but they finally hit the lobby.

Eri handed Willow to one of the other girls and peeked out. "Charlie, what's our status?"

"The lobby seems empty, but just for a moment. I have heat moving that way. If you can get them to run, I highly recommend it. I'll have the limo open and ready."

Eri closed the door and turned to the group. "Listen, I know you're tired and some of you hurt, but I need you to use every ounce of strength you have to run to the entrance. It is currently empty, but we don't know for how long. The sooner we get out of here, the sooner we can get you to safety."

Fear filled their eyes. Most likely, they wondered if they could do this. Eri shared their apprehension. "Myers, you pick up any stragglers. Bryce, you go ahead of us. On the count of three."

"One..." She opened the door. "Two..." She shuffled out of the way to let Bryce by. "Three!"

The group took off running. Myers reached the front door and released it. Charlie waited at the limo, motioning for them to get in. Who knew if it would fit eighteen? Eri reached the door and counted as they dashed by. "Twelve, thirteen, fourteen..."

A team of agents exited the elevator like locust. Guns fired. Glass shattered. Eri pushed the final few out the door, toward the limo. "Charlie, go!" Eri said in her earpiece,

"I'm not leaving you!"

"You have to. There is no room. We'll hold them off."

"But?"

"We'll find you at the apartment. Go!"

Charlie slammed the door, ran to the driver's side,

and pealed out.

Myers, Bryce, and Eri exchanged gunfire, hiding behind the columns at the front of the building.

"We can't lead them to the apartment," Eri said.

"What do you suggest?" Bryce yelled over the battle.

Myers fired one round and then his gun clicked. "I'm out. We have to go."

"Where?" Eri said.

"We'll go to one of the other crack houses," Bryce said.

Eri nodded. She fired a few more shots, and the three took off with every ounce of energy they could muster. Though it was after ten p.m., there was still a lot of traffic. Being on foot could be an advantage.

They ducked down a few alleys.

Eri spotted an open bar and grill. She ducked in. The guys followed. They hurried straight to the back, through to the kitchen. She peeked back out. An agent ran in. A few aprons hung on a hook by the back entrance. She tossed them out to her teammates. They put them on, along with hairnets, and then turned to different parts of the kitchen. A few of the line cooks seemed confused by their presence.

"We were told to help out for the night," Eri simply said.

One cook sent Bryce to clean dishes. Eri was asked to peel potatoes. Myers was sent into the cooler for who knows what.

When the agent poked his head in, Eri made sure to go to the cooler. Bryce must have seen her, because he joined her. The three of them ducked behind boxes of oranges and cabbage. The cooler opened. Eri cocked her gun. The door closed without entry. She shivered. The cold air against her sweaty skin gave her a chill.

"Do you think it is safe?" Myers asked.

"Where are you?" came Charlie's voice in Eri's ear.

"Stuck in the kitchen cooler at McGee's Bar and Grille," she said.

"I'll check it out. Let me log into the cameras."

"Aren't you supposed to get them to safety?" Eri said, annoyed.

"Already done, my sweet."

Eri didn't correct the nickname. She had plenty else to worry about.

"Okay, I'm logged in."

"You really are good at what you do, aren't you?" Eri's teeth chattered.

"S.I.U. didn't come after me for my good looks."

"Nope." Eri laughed. "Too easy."

"Hey, you want me to get you out of there or not?"

"Yes, please." She shivered.

"From what I can see, there are no agents in the bar, but there are no cameras in the kitchen."

Eri relayed what Charlie had said.

"One of us will have to go out," Bryce said.

Myers began walking toward the cooler door. He peered through the window. "I think we're good."

"What are you doing?" a chef said as they started to exit.

Myers laughed. "Man, it's a trip in there. You should try it. Total high."

The chef's face grew red. "Get out of my kitchen!"

"I couldn't agree more." Myers motioned to us to follow him out the back. The limo drove to their position, and they hopped in.

"Are we safe to go to the apartment, or should we circle a bit?" Charlie asked.

"Circle," all three said in union.

Eri lay back on the seat. "Everyone is okay?"

"Yeah, Helena and Alicia are going to help." Charlie turned down an alley and clicked off the lights. They sat in the dark for a moment, listening, waiting. Finally, Charlie started the engine again and backed up.

Myers rubbed a hand over his face. "Those kids are going to need a lot of help, man."

"It was too much." An amber streetlight revealed the tears in Bryce's eyes. He was a tough guy, but even tough guys could break with human compassion.

"That was us not long ago," Charlie said.

"What a difference a year makes." Eri closed her eyes. She willed all of this away. They had broken into S.I.U. and chose a battle over the war. Compassion had stopped them from their main objective. But who could blame them? Eighteen more souls were no longer lost.

Chapter Twenty-Nine

Laura woke to the chattering of unfamiliar voices. Light shined through the windows, casting an orange hue on the stained ceiling. She rolled over to find the tiny apartment filled with wall-to-wall teenagers sitting around the room eating what looked like cups of noodles.

"Well, hello there." A boy with white-blond hair and a smile way too chipper for this moment stared back at her. "I'm Theodore Ronald, the Third. My parents had this thing for presidents. I mean, we do live in Washington D.C. after all. But I guess I can be glad I wasn't called Garfield. He's a cat. But my friends call me Teddy. I decided you can call me that, too. Hungry? I made everyone lunch. I think there is a beef flavor still left. I can get it for you, if you'd like."

"Lunch?" Laura stretched up from the corner by the kitchenette and glanced around. Her muscles ached from the beating and sleeping on what looked like Charlie's shoes. "What time is it?"

"A little after one p.m. You slept a lot. Not that anyone can blame you. I don't. That's for sure…"

She held up her hand. This boy was sweet, but he could talk. It didn't help that her head ached. The night before blurred in her memory. A vague thought of being shot with drugs lingered. After that—nothing. There were no recognizable faces in the room, and a slight panic resonated in her mind. Who were these kids? And why were they in her apartment. "Where is my team?"

The boy pointed to the door. "They are conversing in the hallway. It was too crowded, and they said they had some tough decisions to make. I think we were too chatty for them to really be able to discuss anything."

Laura tried to stand, but her legs wobbled under her.

"Oh here, let me help you." He reached his arm under hers. "I'm Teddy by the way."

"You said that."

"Right. Sorry."

"I'm Laura."

"Black, yeah, we know." People shifted so they could walk by, each stopped talking to watch her. "You're kind of a celebrity of sorts. All of us grew up being told about you. Or I should say, being told not to end up like you." He chuckled a contagious laugh. "Of course, as you can see, we were all locked up, so we obviously ignored that rule."

Laura faced him. "Locked up?"

"Oh, you don't remember, do you?"

She shook her head.

"We were kidnapped to be S.I.U. agents, but we all messed up one way or another. I was locked up for over a month. That girl on the end, Kelsey, she was locked up for a whole year. Not sure why they didn't terminate her. Not sure why they didn't terminate all of us. There were some people who were only there a day, and they disappeared. Glad to not be them, but it does make you wonder. You know?"

Call it a long night or just plain anger—emotion

poured out in tears along Laura's cheeks. They would never stop. If Kelsey had been there a year, that meant about the time they locked up Greenstone, she was being locked away, too. Each part of this had only been a kick in the side of a large meat-eating dinosaur. They had only riled the trees. Nothing had damaged the enemy. Now, it would be open season on her team. They had rescued people for what? There would be retaliation. What had they done?

Teddy opened the door and helped her out.

The team sat at the top of the stairs down the hall. Bryce saw her and rushed to her side. "I'll take it from here, kid. Thanks."

"Sure thing. Need anything else."

"Everyone fed?" Bryce asked.

The boy nodded with a proud grin.

"Then go relax. You earned it." He patted Teddy's back and then turned to help Laura down the hall.

Teddy watched for a moment and then ducked back inside.

Laura lowered herself onto the top step. Every bone screamed for surrender. "What's going on?"

"We had to pick our battle last night, but it may have been a possible wrong move," Myers said.

Eri scowled. "It was not the wrong move. Those kids were ready to die in there."

"We didn't win the war. They'll come after us, Eri. We were supposed to damage them. But instead, we just gave away our position." Myers jumped up and started pacing in the hall. "Rescue them from what? All we did was prolong their fate."

"Look, I had to make a call. And you could have stopped me, but you helped because you knew it was right." Her voice cracked with emotion.

Laura got it. Seeing those kids broke her heart, too, but they should have waited until it could all happen at once. "Okay, stop. You're both right and wrong here. Fighting will not help."

Both of them stared at her.

"It was right to rescue them. I just think the timing was a little off." Laura shifted to get a more comfortable position. "Myers is accurate. We gave our position away, but I saw that one girl in there with red hair. She wasn't going to make it another day."

"Fine, but what do we do now?" Myers spat.

"We do what we always do." Laura smiled. "Improvise."

It took a second, but the group returned her grin.

An uproarious popping sounded in the other room. The team leapt to their feet and ran to the door. Fear gripped Laura as she inched after them and was the last to the door. Cries lifted from the room. Gunfire shredded the walls. Laura's throat tensed, and a heat pulsed through her. Several kids lay in pools of blood on the floor, clenching porous wounds, or eternally paralyzed. The others scrounged for protection against the corners of the room, and a few lay prone, futilely pulling at the carpet.

"Everyone in the hall," Eri screeched.

The team ripped the kids from their sanctuaries and picked up those who hugged the ground. Once the kids were in the hall, Myers and Bryce dipped into the room, trading fire with the assailants.

Laura held back the group from getting close to the staircase. This was their last stand. Their numbers were too small to handle the agents if they made it up the stairs, and the other room was a kill zone. Prayer. If there was ever a time, it was now. A concoction of doubt, anger, and desperation mixed in her mind. Words of feverous prayer trampled her thoughts. But a booming declaration raced the voice of hope. This was an impossible moment. Did they rescue all of them, only to see them crucified for running?

Several agents charged into view. This was it. Laura clenched her jaw and whipped her gun toward them. Eri tugged the others to the ground. Sweat drenched Laura's neck. Her finger began to depress the trigger. The agents flew to the ground, blood spurting from behind them. Laura froze. The trigger of her weapon was still in mid fire, not a bullet had left. More gunshots rang in the hall.

A silence permeated the room. The gunfire had stopped.

A victorious call came from the lower room, "The cavalry has arrived," Charlie championed.

Another figure appeared in the stairway. Laura once again readied her gun. Antonio Dubois stepped over the bodies and strutted to her location. "So your baby killers tried to take one of my soldiers this morning. We followed them here. Figured this was our fight too."

In that moment, Laura could have kissed him.

"You just saved our lives. I don't even know what to say."

He shrugged. "It's all about scratching backs when its time. But seriously, this was personal. No one takes my guy and lives to tell about it. So we're in." He pulled a gold pen from the lining of his cheap suit and a small pad from his pocket. "What do you need?"

****

Laura watched as Antonio had a cleaner take both the bodies of the three dead kids, as well as the bodies of the dead agents. The quality of the neighborhood was magnified by the fact no cops had come, even though there had been plenty of gunfire. Still hard to believe they were only a mile from the Capitol. The level of poverty was astounding.

"We have to relocate," Laura said to everyone. "Grab whatever you can carry. Let's start down the steps."

One girl with red hair sobbed almost uncontrollably. Laura was not good with consoling people. She tapped Teddy on the back.

"Crazy, huh? I am just so—"

She held up a hand to interrupt him. "Do you think you could help her?"

His gaze followed Laura's. "Oh, Willow, yeah sure."

"Thank you."

That was a great kid. He still held a spark that not many of them had. She hoped it remained burning bright. Better yet, she hoped they could finish this before the water of jade came and rained on his parade.

The team and new group of teens gathered all they could and hurried to the limo. They stopped, but didn't get in. Laura started to ask why, when she saw why. It was riddled with bullets and the tires all flat. This vehicle was not taking them anywhere. She spun around and gave a tight smile to Myers.

"I'm going shopping?" he said knowingly.

"Yup."

He turned to Helena and grinned. "Wanna come?"

"Sure. I've never boosted a car before." She laughed.

The two disappeared around the corner, and Laura surveyed the area. They couldn't stay here. A huge bull's-eye was on their backs. Not to mention, she could barely stand.

"We can go to that donut shop down the street. There we can keep an eye on things, while waiting," Eri said.

Laura nodded.

Bryce must have read her mind. He wrapped her arm around his neck and lifted her with other. Together, they walked to the end of the block to the donut shop. Inside, the room smelled of sugar.

Charlie treated everyone to donut holes and coffee. Eri stood post at the door. Alicia took over for Teddy as counselor, holding Willow's hand and rubbing her head. The two were close in age. It almost seemed like they had been best friends for years, but more likely, they shared tragedy. That bond could often go deeper than blood.

After over an hour wait, the shop owner started to look annoyed. Laura hoped Myers would return soon. Just when Laura was about to apologize to the owner, a moving truck pulled up in front of the apartment complex. *He really has a knack for finding the weirdest transportation.* "Let's go."

The group piled out and crossed the street.

"A moving truck?" Laura asked when they reached them.

He held up his hands. "Look, we couldn't find much. This was the best we could do. Most the vehicles are new, and you know we can't take anything with a tracker. And there just aren't a lot of vans around here."

"You could have got another limo," Charlie said. "Lots of those."

"Don't you think if we stole a senator's limo, someone would come looking for it?"

"Touché," Charlie said.

"Okay, everyone in the back," Laura said, then frowned at Myers. "If we get pulled over, we're going to look like human traffickers."

"It's just temporary until we find new digs."

The group filed in, and Laura shut the door with fifteen recued teens, Charlie, Myers, Helena, and Alicia inside. Bryce decided to drive with Laura and Eri in front to discuss strategy.

The problem was they didn't have one. "We need to contact Dubois. Maybe he can help us."

"I agree. I think that may be our only way to win this war." Bryce pulled over to a booth by the side of the road. "Get a burner phone."

Eri jumped out and walked to the booth. She purchased the phone and returned to the truck. Laura contacted him, and he gave her an address. They drove for ten minutes, before arriving at a loading dock.

Bryce backed in.

Laura jumped out and slid the back door up. Everyone piled out onto the dock.

A man with a rifle stepped outside the door. "What are you doing here?"

Laura held her hands open in front of her. "Antonio Dubois sent us."

"Name?"

"Laura Black."

The guy pulled a cell phone from his pocket and

radioed someone. It beeped and the person on the other line confirmed it. "Okay. Come on."

The band of young adults followed the man through a metal door, through an open bay filled with cars and mechanics. The room buzzed with drills and lit with sparks, as people chopped the likely boosted cars. The man turned around several times to make sure they followed close. In the back lay a large room filled with cushy, red couches decorated with cowhide pillows and fur blankets. Dubois sat on a single chair across from them like a king, petting a ferret in the crook of his arm. It was almost surreal how trite it was.

"Go ahead. Sit wherever." He waved at them as they entered. "You know, I don't let a lot of people in here." His gaze locked with Laura's. "But I trust you. You will keep that trust, am I right?"

"Without a doubt. We are sorry to impose, but honestly, we are at our wits' end." Laura glanced over at Myers and then Eri. They nodded for her to continue. "We can't leave Maryland until we have taken this evil cancer down. But we're depleted. We need help."

"See as we have a shared enemy, I'm okay helping." He sat the ferret down, and it ducked under his arm and down the back of the chair. "But I don't do much for free. I have a business to run and reputation to maintain. I've seen you all. You're hardcore. I like that. But you promised me something. I need to know I will get it."

"You mean the file at the F.B.I.?" Laura asked.

"For certainty, my dear. That was the deal."

Laura shot Charlie a look. He didn't give her any indication he would or wouldn't do it, but he would be her only hope. "When we are done with S.I.U., and have more freedom to be on the street without being made by them, we will make that our first priority. You have my word or my life."

Bryce grabbed her hand. No, she wasn't going to allow him to speak into this.

Deal?" she asked.

Antonio clapped his hands together and howled.

Laura had never met anyone like him. She hoped her face gave nothing away on how awkward he made her feel.

"Then, missy, I think I can help you."

Chapter Thirty

Myers loaded the last cartridge into a black duffle bag. His spirits were rising. With the help of the Dubois crew, they had a fighting chance. Laura had mentioned if they didn't hurry, though, the entire S.I.U. building would be vacated. The protocol was forty-eight hours after being compromised. It had been almost twenty-four.

There was no time to sleep. Each kicked back some caffeine pills and was ready to go. Antonio's team sniffed other substances. Laura played her mother role, making sure no one on her team snorted anything. Didn't bother Myers. He never used. He had seen many family members O.D. over the years. It wasn't worth it.

Myers stared at the dozen young people packing guns and sharpening knives a few feet away. The distant expressions worried him. He pulled Laura and Bryce aside. "Are you sure those kids are ready? Only a few of them are trained, and of those, most of them are still healing from torture. They look more like zombies than soldiers."

"What other choice do we have?" Laura asked. "We just aren't big enough to take down that entire place without them. There are probably one hundred or more agents in that building. I still don't know how we got out so easily the other night."

"We just saved them. I don't want anybody else to

die." Myers rubbed a hand over his face and walked away.

Helena sat in the corner by a water fountain filling canteens. He grabbed a chair and pulled it next to her. "You okay?"

"A little shook up from this morning." She shook her head and sniffed. "One girl was only a foot from me when she fell. Bullet right through the eye."

He tucked a strand of hair behind her ear and kissed her forehead. "It doesn't ever get easier, but hopefully, this will be where it ends."

"I want them to pay."

An emotion Myers knew all too well. Flashbacks of Denise being shot the same way as this young girl were still evident almost every moment of his waking hour. Not one of them deserved to be here—fighting for their right to live an ordinary life. There was possibly a chance to rehabilitate them. At least, Laura seemed to think so.

It had been determined that the older ones would likely not be able to turn, and shoot to kill would be okay, if need be. But the younger ones…? Laura said to save them if possible. Simply kidnap them back. That would not be easy. Would they put their own lives in danger to try and help them? And more importantly, where did they take them? He let go of Helena. "I'll be right back." He crossed to where Laura was cleaning a weapon. "Laura, we have to talk strategy. We have no place to keep fifty kids."

"Yeah." She set the weapon on a towel and faced him. "I have decided what to do. Gather everyone up."

Finally. He liked action; he was never one for waiting. It took just a minute or so for Myers to get everyone to circle up on the cement floor. Laura stood in the hole of the circle.

"First, if you are not well enough to go, we need to know. We will have some of Antonio's guys and all of my team, so no unnecessary risks. If that's you, please raise your hand." She peered around the group. Willow was clearly not in a place to go. Hunched over, she held her stomach. It actually may be time to get her to the doctor. "You need to stay here, okay?"

Willow bobbed her head once and then lay to the floor.

Laura looked at Helena. "Is there any way you can get her to the urgent care? I saw one up the street on the left."

"Is that safe?" Bryce asked.

"No, probably not. But something is wrong with her. Either way, it's not good."

Helena leaned down and picked her up. Her frail body couldn't have weighed more than sixty pounds. The two of them walked out the side door and into the alley. Myers hated to see Helena go. What if something happened to her? He had to shake that off. Too much at stake.

Laura turned back to the group. The expressions of the kids were a mix of fear and anger. Myers understood that.

"So, the idea is that we take down all S.I.U. leaders." Laura paced. "If you find a young kid, you lock them up in the jail you all came out of. We keep them there for safekeeping. If they are in there, they are safe. So, the more we can round up, the better."

The group of teens all shared their approval through nods or verbal understanding.

"I know this will be hard. Some of you trained with these people. The older agents are conditioned. Turning them will be almost impossible. Do not hesitate to bring them down. If you do, they will not hesitate to shoot you."

The group mumbled and groaned.

"Okay, quiet down. Listen. There are some dangerous operatives there. Especially Harding." The room fell silent. "I know he is there. He used to be my partner. I know how good he is. If you see him…" She glanced around the entire group, probably making sure her gaze fell to each person. "Do not engage. Radio Charlie."

"Will we have radios?" Teddy asked.

"We only have five for all of you. You will need to get in groups of three. The rest of us are on coms. We'll show you how to reach Charlie, so he can get us. Questions?"

Everyone murmured, a few hands rose, but then quickly lowered.

Finally, Teddy asked, "When do we leave?"

"In an hour."

Chapter Thirty-One

Eri helped load the last piece of equipment where Charlie had set up a temporary office in the back of the moving truck. She kissed his cheek and moved to walk away. He caught her arm and pulled her back. His lips lightly touched hers. "You be safe in there."

"I will be, because you've got my back." She ran a hand along the side of his cheek as she walked to the edge of the truck and jumped down. The team was ready to go. All of the rescued teens were now dressed in city black and gray camo that Antonio stole from some paintball store. Guns were distributed, as were gasmasks, grenades, and walkie talkies.

"Let's go," Laura said, coming out from the building.

All of them loaded inside the truck and sat on the floor. Eri sat closest to the front. One of Antonio's men slammed the door closed and pounded on the back. Myers was in the driver's seat. The engine revved and left the lot. The back bounced and rattled. Anytime they turned, the group fell into one another. Some people prayed. Others sat silent and wide-eyed. There had been no time to assess their skills. It was impossible to know if they could do this or not. The best they had was the amount of time they had been in S.I.U. The shortest was only a few months. The longest two years.

The truck stopped. Eri stood, and the others

followed suit. The clank of guns lifting from the floor sounded around her. The door sprang open. Myers, Laura, Bryce, and ten of Antonio's men stood in front of her. The gang was a menacing group. She was glad they were on her side.

"We walk in groups from here," Laura said.

Only Charlie stayed behind. Eri touched her ear as shewaved. "I love you, you know?"

"Ditto, sweetheart."

She shook her head, but smiled.

"Come back to me, okay?"

"Promise." She ran off with Teddy and another guy name Deshawn, and Antonio's guy—Daiki. Each person from the team would partner up with two or three kids and one Dubois crewmember.

Her group all said they could climb walls. Teddy swore he used to go mountain climbing before S.I.U. Deshawn had the highest rating in parkour at the academy. Though Daiki didn't explain why he was with her, just looking at his thin frame, he looked the part.

Eri ran at the wall and pushed off, jumping as she did, landing against a railing and pulling herself up. She swung to a windowsill and shifted along it until she could reach the rope she had mounted the last time she was here. She locked in and then tossed the end down to the other two. Belaying up the side of building proved tougher this time. Maybe because of the urgency. Her uncle often said that an anxious mind would stop action. She inhaled through her nose and exhaled slowly through her mouth. *Focus, Eri. Forget the end goal, and focus on the action.* It worked. When she reached the top, she untied and checked her gun. Locked, but loaded.

Teddy and Deshawn swung over the side, then Daiki flipped over into a stance. Instantly, she knew his style. Kendo. He would come in handy.

They moved with purpose to the air vent. "Charlie, we're ready for you to disconnect the lasers."

"Already done."

They dropped in, shimmed down, and crawled to the opening grate she had used before. The office wasn't empty. A woman shredded papers from a box. A man rushed in, grabbed something, and then rushed out.

Eri pointed to her eyes and then to the room.

Daiki nodded and held a finger to his lips. He motioned for Eri to move and then lowered himself behind the woman at the shredder with ninja agility and grace. He withdrew a tiny can from his pocket and sprayed it at her face. She dropped probably before being able to discern what happened. Daiki set her down under the desk and scooted the chair in.

Deshawn and Teddy dropped down.

The rushing guy came in and stopped short. Mouth open, he turned to go. Teddy leapt over a chair and tackled him, keeping a hand over his mouth. Daiki walked next to him and sprayed the toxin. The man went limp.

Teddy smiled ear-to-ear.

Eri offered a closed mouth smile. This kid was too much. She used a mirrored device to peer down the hall. Nothing. "Clear," she mouthed.

They checked each office. A few people lingered, destroying files or equipment. But no Harding. Their job was simple. Quietly find Harding. Capture him and bring him back. The rest of the team had a more deliberated execution. Bring down S.I.U. brick by brick, leader by leader. All young teens were to be locked up and rehabilitated. They ran for the service elevator.

At the end of the hall, Eri spotted Myers tossing two teens into a cell. She nodded and ran by to hit the button going down. They would check each floor if they had to. Her com buzzed. "Charlie?" she whispered. "What's up?"

"I found him through one of the cameras. He's on the sixth floor."

"What's there? What's he doing?"

"That's the armory. I'll give you one guess."

Eri closed her eyes and breathed out. "Okay."

"Be careful."

Eri glanced at the other two. "He's in the armory."

Teddy rolled his eyes.

Daiki nodded. "Floor?"

"Sixth."

They pushed the fifth and seventh floor and then climbed through an opening in the roof of the elevator. The four held on, as it slid down the square tunnel. When it started to pass the sixth floor, Eri, Deshawn, and Daiki jumped. Teddy waited and had to jump to a ladder just below it.

"You okay?" Eri said.

He nodded and reached out a hand.

Daiki and Eri pulled him up. All four of them balanced on a small ledge. Daiki used a tool to slowly open the door, enough to peek out. Voices could be heard behind the wall. He opened a slit large enough for them to maneuver through, then followed before closing the gap. They slunk across to the wall. Sounds of guns being loaded into what sounded like a trunk or crate.

Eri and Deshawn went right. Daiki and Teddy crawled left.

Peeking around the wall, it was evident they were out gunned. Agent after agent walked in and was handed a gun. Luckily, they were entering and exiting in a "U" formation, not approaching her location.

Eri peered across the way. Teddy's white blond hair barely visible. No sign of Daiki.

With all these agents here, Eri didn't know what to do.

"Gas mask on," came Charlie's voice.

Eri glanced at Deshawn.

"I heard," Deshawn said, pulling his mask out.

Eri pulled hers out and spun around the wall, crawling fast to Teddy. By the time she reached him, she had hers on. His eyes went wide, and he pulled his out. Hopefully, Daiki got the message too.

Yes. His shadow fell on the rafter above her. He was about to expose the team to some kind of agent.

Eri's goggles fogged up a bit. She tried to still her breathing to avoid any condensation.

Coughing, bodies collapsed. Eri peered out again. Everyone, including Harding, lay on the ground. Eri ran to his side and pulled her gun from her holster. Every part of her soul screamed to put it to his head and squeeze the trigger. This man killed her best friend. This monster murdered Helena's father, not to mention the many other lives that were still hurting because he could not let S.I.U. go.

"No, don't." Teddy touched her hand. "Not here. Not now. Laura said."

Eri heard the words, but they almost didn't

compute.

Deshawn reached past her, flipped him over, and bound his hands. He tossed him over his shoulder and walked toward the elevator. "What about the rest of them?" Eri asked Charlie on her com.

"Clean-up crew behind you. No worries. Just get Harding out."

"Roger." She turned to the group. "Let's go." Each of them grabbed a gun and then followed. They took it to the twelfth floor. To their left was an arrow that said, "roof."

Teddy ran to it and climbed the ladder. "There's an opening." He hit the small lock a few times with the butt of his gun, and it popped off. He climbed up, then Eri. Both of them reached down to pull up Harding. The man was heavy. They pulled him through the hole and onto the roof. Once outside, Eri removed her mask. A light snow began to filter through the air. They had to hurry.

Deshawn reached the top and grabbed Harding again. Good thing, too, or he might have fallen off the roof. Eri smiled at that thought.

They tied him to the rope and lowered him down. Once they were all on the ground, Deshawn picked him up again, and they proceeded to the truck a few blocks away.

Charlie had prepared a place for him. Once there, they chained him to a hook on the wall, usually used to ground furniture. When he woke, chances are he'd be furious. No matter. If it were up to her, being angry would be the least of his worries.

"Do we go back or stay with the package?" Teddy asked.

"Someone has to stay, but they could likely use our help." Eri glanced at Charlie. "How are they doing?"

"Fifty-fifty. They could use a hand, but more than that, you have to secure those weapons."

Eri placed a hand on Teddy's shoulder. "You stay here and guard Harding with your life. If anyone, and I mean anyone who is not with us, tries to come take him, shoot him or her on sight. Understand?"

Teddy nodded fervently.

"Good." Eri waved to Charlie and joined Daiki and Deshawn on the run back.

Chapter Thirty-Two

Myers reached down and grabbed an older guy by the neck. The man walked up the wall and flipped back to face Myers. He punched, knocking Myers back. He shook his head to clear the daze. The guy reached for a knife on the table. Myers turned his arms in, to block any major arteries, and prepared for the worse. The guy stabbed at the air. Myers kicked at his side.

The guy stumbled back, but recovered quickly. He stabbed again, this time slicing Myers shirt. Myers spun around and dropped kicked him in the face. The guy fell hard against the wall, but was still slightly coherent. Without hesitation, Myers wrapped the crook of his arm around the guy's neck and pulled with all his might. The man fought, and it took every muscle to hold on.

Emotion passed through Myer's body. He could not take another life without feeling the experience himself. This man would come after them. There was no doubt of that fact. He had to die. But it still hurt. If only they could abide by the law. Lock him up. But S.I.U. was bigger than the system. With moles in the government and police stations, the man would be out before the ink was dry on their forms. *Another kid killer back on the street.* The only cure for this disease rested in the crook of Myers' arm. It saddened him, but it was the only way.

The guy fell limp.

Slowly, Myers scrammed out from under him and staggered to the next room. Two agents fought the two teens who had come with him. From the looks of it, the agents were winning. Blood seeped from the kids' noses, and one of them had a swollen eye.

One agent reached in his back for a gun.

Myers fired. The agent dropped. He fired again. The second agent dropped.

The kids slumped to the floor, nursing their wounds.

"Are you okay?" Myers asked.

Neither responded. The proof was in the blood.

"You need to get out of here and back to the truck. Make sure you aren't followed."

The two nodded, leaned on each other, and teetered out the door.

Myers darted to the next office. Empty. The next. Empty. He started to enter the last one, when something shifted to his left. His heart pounded. He turned, gun in hand. *Laura.* "You scared me."

"Sorry. All the floors are cleared."

"Any casualties?"

Her face grew somber. "Yeah, four more of ours were killed."

"Who?"

She shook her head. "I didn't know their names."

"The good news, we found about thirty other kids who weren't full blown agents yet. They are locked up like you wanted." Myers walked to a desk and sat on top. "Now what?"

Laura grabbed the nameplate from the desk and dropped it in the trashcan. "Once it is secure, I'll contact the authorities."

He furrowed his eyebrow. "I thought we couldn't do that."

"It's a risk, yeah, but no way can we keep these kids. They need to go back to their families."

That spawned an idea. "Maybe if we give them each a phone, they'll start calling themselves. Witnesses. People they trust."

"That's brilliant." Laura hit his arm and lifted her burner from her back pocket. "Do you have yours?"

"Yeah, here." He handed his out.

"Come on." They walked to the lock up and to the end. Instead of the heavy doors, Myers had only pulled the bars. "Look, guys, I know you're confused and angry, but we're really here to help."

"If you want to help us, let us out," one girl said.

Laura shook her head. "I can't. Not yet."

"Why not?" Another asked.

"Because, honestly, we don't trust you." Laura held up the phone. "My friend and I both have phones. If you behave, we're going to give them to you to call home. To let your folks know where you are and that you're okay."

"Really?" a girl said, voice cracking.

"Really. On one condition."

They jammed against the bars. "What's that?" one said.

"If there is anyone in there with you that would call anyone but their family, we need to know now." Laura glanced around, and Myers followed suit.

The group all looked at each other, the expression on their faces said volumes as it settled on a tall guy with a shaved head, his eyes piercing, a perpetual scowl. Myers knew that look. Who put him in here? He was hardly going to be rehabilitated.

"If no one tells me, no one calls," Laura said.

An African-American girl with short hair pointed at the guy. "Jesse is total diehard S.I.U. Only been here a month, but he'd die for them, for sure. No doubt."

"That's right. I would." He sauntered up to the bars, and the group paved a way like the Red Sea. "You are all a bunch of losers. Caving into what? To go back to parents who didn't want us. We belong here. We had a purpose. I will not let you ruin this."

"Yeah, a purpose to kill innocent people," Laura said.

"Judge not, lest you be judged—Agent Black!"

Laura raised an eyebrow, crossing to where he stood. "So you know me?" She glanced back at Myers. He knew what she was thinking. How did this kid know her name?

"Yeah, that's right. I know you. We all do. Your picture was used in target practice many times. We were told you are the enemy. Still are." He spit in her face. "You're a traitor. You deserve to die."

Without blinking, she wiped the spittle from her face with the back of her sleeve. "You're an imbecile. Myers."

Myers held the gun at the guy's head and pulled. Everyone screamed. Jesse touched the side of his head. His ear bled, but he was still alive. "You missed."

"No, that's called a warning. I never miss." Myers locked his gun and stuffed it back in his waistline.

"Now let's try this again." Laura stood at a casual parade rest. "I was you. I grew up in this organization. I would have killed for them, too. But I learned the truth—that you are just being used to do their dirty work. This place…" She spanned her arms out. "It's not real. There is no black ops organization for the government that employees kids. As ridiculous as it sounds, it is."

One girl lifted herself up and pressed her cheek to the bar. "So this isn't legal?"

Myers laughed. "Hardly."

"But they promised me—."

Laura reached to her. "They promised all of us."

Myers looked back to Jesse. His head was down, so there was no way to know for sure if they should trust him. They needed to separate him. Myers lifted his gun and walked to the jail door.

Laura lifted hers and aimed it, too.

"Let's go, Jesse."

Jesse's eyes met his. "I won't cause trouble. I'm sorry for spitting."

"We can't take that chance. Come on, now, or the next bullet will be in your brain." Myers swung the door open enough for him to exit. He didn't waste time shutting it again, but keeping the gun on the back of the guy's head. "Move."

Two steps and Jesse spun around and tried to knock the gun from Myers's hand. Luckily, Myers had anticipated it and fired. The bullet shot through Jesse's right shoulder. He fell back to the ground holding the wound.

Laura opened another cell at the front.

Myers shoved him in and slammed it closed. "Thanks for proving our point."

"You can't keep me in here. I'll bleed to death."

Laura offered a creepy smile and walked back to the cells on the end.

"We're counting on it," Myers said, before joining her. Not really. First, the bullet went all the way through. Second, Laura would call the authorities, and he'd likely be rescued in time. But for right now, it was almost enjoyable to see him squirm.

Myers and Laura passed the phones through the bars.

The teens gobbled them up like a prized gift. One-by-one, they called, crying. Most didn't even know what part of the world they were in. Likely transported with blindfolds, just like they had been so long ago.

With each call, Myers choked up more. *This was for you, Denise,* he thought. The joy in that moment outweighed so much pain. They had saved at least thirty or more kids. Within an hour or so, every person had called someone.

"What now?" one girl asked.

"We'll call the authorities, and they will take you home." Laura took her phone back and dialed 9-1-1 as they moved to the elevator. "Yes, there are a bunch of teenagers locked up in an office building at 16659 North West Broadway. Try the twelfth floor." Laura snapped the phone closed and glanced at Myers, before running for the exit.

He joined her as they jogged back the few blocks to the truck. They had done it. No guarantees that their future was free, but for now, it looked much brighter.

Chapter Thirty-Three

Laura stared deep into Harding's brown eyes. Cold and distant, she hardly recognized the man before her. He had shaved all of his hair, making him appear more menacing. Possessed by power, he had allowed the organization to turn him into the thing they hated—another Greenstone. Though she doubted she could break him, she had to try. She walked around the metal chair that sat in the middle of Antonio's warehouse, deciding what to do next.

Myers punched him in the jaw again. A trickle of blood ran from a slice in his cheek.

"Hey, dummy." Harding smiled through the blood on his lip and teeth. "This won't work, you know. I've had many years of P.O.W. training. Laura knows this. You are just wasting your time and energy."

"Oh, I'm sure that's true. This isn't about that." Myers grinned a sardonic grin. "This is about making me feel better."

"Is it working?" Laura played along.

"A little." Myers winked.

"Why? Because I killed your girlfriend?"

Myers punched him again, much harder. Blood squirted from his around his eye to the cement floor. Hopefully Antonio wouldn't care about the blood. Chances are this floor had seen blood before.

Harding blinked to clear his sight. "I'm sorry, but

someone had to pay for what you did."

Laura held Myers back and faced him. "And what was that exactly?"

"You are so stupid, Black. I had no plans of coming after your team." Harding sneered. "But no, you couldn't leave well enough alone. You had to push it, and in doing so, I had no choice but to retaliate."

"What are you talking about?" Myers leaned in.

"I'm talking about you guys breaking into Madison and Clark, our shell company. You could have lived the rest of your lives without ever seeing us again, but you stole from us instead." He spat at the floor. "That we couldn't allow."

Guilt flooded Laura's chest. She shot Myers a look of apology. That had been her call. How could she know they were free? She had just assumed that if S.I.U. had a shell company, they had to do something to protect themselves. It never occurred to her they would be waking the giant.

Myers eyes narrowed. His face grew crimson. The fury and pain that resonated on his face made her fearful he might actually hit her this time. She would let him. It was her fault Denise died. How could she have been so stupid? How could she have let this happen? Would Myers ever be able to forgive her?

"I'm sorry," she mouthed.

He began to pace around the chair, something he often did when he was angry. Suddenly, he stopped and spun on his heel to face Harding. "How many kids have you taken just this year?"

Harding shrugged. "At least a hundred. I don't know. Who cares? It's just business."

Myers greeted Laura's gaze. "You have nothing to

apologize for, Black. This was bigger than our freedom or just one life. It is a cause we would all die for. Denise included."

Harding laughed. "How noble."

Myers backhanded him and Harding's head dropped unconscious.

"Good. He was giving me a headache." Laura reached for Myers and hugged him tight. She pulled back and stared him in the eye. "It was my call back then. Whether it was right or not, I am still sorry."

He squeezed her, pulled back, and said, "No. We are here today, having rescued at least thirty or more kids. I can live with that." He circled Harding, glaring at him. "What I'm not okay with is this piece of garbage being free in any capacity. What do you propose we do with him?"

"I don't know." Her brain just couldn't fill in the gap. "If he lives, he will build again. If he dies, it may solve one problem, but I never really like taking the life of an unarmed man. It doesn't seem right." Laura sat on a chair across from him and let out a deep sigh. "To be honest, I'm not sure what to do with him."

Bryce walked in through the side door off the alley and joined them in the warehouse. He stepped behind her and began to massage her shoulders. Slowly, he leaned down to her ear. "Where are we with everything?"

"Myers knocked him out." She grinned.

"I see that. Good job, my friend. Must have felt good."

Myers beamed. "It did."

Bryce walked around to face her, bending to her level. "I meant, what are we going to do with him?"

"Funny, that is what we were just discussing." Laura stood, wrapping her arm behind his back. "Ideas?"

Bryce pinched his lips together and exhaled. "It has to be permanent, whatever we do. That much is obvious."

"I have an idea," Helena said from the doorway.

All eyes shifted to her.

She walked toward them. "What if we locked him away in a nut house like they did *The Count of Monte Cristo*."

"Or t*he Man in the Iron Mask*." Bryce let go of Laura and smiled. "That's an awesome idea."

Myers and Laura glanced at each other.

"The who and who?" she said.

Bryce laughed. "My uncultured wife. Both stories are about people who were locked away where no one knew who they were. Hidden forever from society."

"I like the word forever. But how do we lock Harding away?"

Helena grinned. "We create a really good story."

Chapter Thirty-Four

Eri stepped to a mirror in Antonio's office and pushed the black glasses higher on her nose. She could tell by Charlie's goofy grin in the reflection that he liked the "nerd" look. She smiled turning to him. "So, do I look like a doctor?"

"Sure." He pulled her into a hug and whispered in her ear. "A hot doctor."

She playfully pushed him back. "Do you have my credentials?"

Charlie handed out a black wallet and a file. "The transfer orders are inside."

She took both, hoping she could pull this off. Laura was the better actor. Why they decided it be her, she was unsure.

"You okay?"

She looked up from the wallet and met his stare. His soft green eyes held concern and love. She touched his cheek and offered a closed-mouth grin. "I'm just nervous. You know this isn't my forte. I would rather be kicking someone in the head or climbing up the side of a building."

He laughed. "Yes, I can see that."

"Why me?"

Charlie leaned toward her and opened the wallet. Inside was an Asian woman who was not an exact match. "Without much time, we boosted a real badge."

The light went on. She nodded.

Laura and Bryce walked in dressed in security guard costumes, holding a bound and hooded Harding. They directed him toward a van Myers had absconded just that morning.

Helena and Alicia waved to them as the team climbed inside. They waved back and then waited for one of Antonio's men to lift the warehouse door. They decided to take a back route, just in case some other agents would come looking for him. It only took twenty minutes outside the city to reach their destination. A sign at a gated entrance read, "Forest View Mental Health Facility." Myers pulled along a guard shack.

From the passenger seat, Eri held up her badge and passed over the file. "I'm here to deliver a patient."

The guard looked over the transfer order and passed it back. "Take him to the west end entrance."

"Thank you," Eri said, taking the file back.

Myers rolled the window up and pulled forward. A three-story brick building lay to their right. An open trail surrounded the outside with limited trees and bushes. The windows were barred and covered. The van stopped just outside a double-door marked, "Admittance."

Eri undid her seat belt and spun to face them. "Is he good?"

Laura reached under hood and checked the earplugs and gag on Harding. She nodded. "Let's do it."

Once the van stopped, Eri got out on the passenger side and pushed back the sliding door. Bryce and Laura pushed him forward and out. Surprisingly, he didn't fight them. He probably knew at this point, it wouldn't work.

They marched him to the west door and hit a call button on the side. A nurse walked to the window. Eri held up badge. The door buzzed open, and they entered.

"I have a pretty troubled patient. He's has become a danger to himself and others." Eri lifted the hood. "He's suffering with dissociative identity disorder and hallucinations. He thinks he's a secret agent, among other things. He's really just a janitor at an elementary school. Single, no family. Not many people will miss him. Here is the judge's order for him to have mandatory care." Eri handed over the file and held her breath.

"And why the ear plugs and gag."

"I was trying to keep the stimuli to a minimum." Eri glanced at him. "He can change demeanor very fast."

The nurse scanned the page and nodded. "This way."

She led them down a long corridor. Half-comatose people stared at them from the rooms as they walked back. Laura had chosen this place for their positive regard for keeping patients heavy medicated. She led them to a room with a table and straps. Two orderlies were inside. One held a syringe. The other stood with crossed arms, probably to see if there would be an issue.

Harding's eyes went wide. The reality of his situation probably just clicked. He began to thrash. Laura and Bryce tried to hold him. A large orderly walked to the left with the syringe, and the other one came to their assistance. Together, they pushed him toward the table. The syringe jammed into his neck. Harding stilled. They lifted him up, and the other orderly secured straps on his wrists and ankles.

"I can see he'll try to be a handful, but we deal with his kind every day. No worries."

"Be aware, he is very dangerous. He has been known to strike out violently and hurt people. Do not underestimate him," Eri said. "I would recommend sedation."

A doctor walked in. The nurse handed him the file. He scanned it and then signed it. "We'll take it from here."

Eri shook his hand and started to walk out, when she remembered one last detail. "Just so you know, he has threatened to kill his fellow employees. If he gets out of here, that will be the first place he goes."

The doctor pursed his lips. "Don't worry. He's not going anywhere."

It took everything she had for Eri not to scream out a "halleluiah." Instead, Eri remained calm, nodded, and exited with Laura and Bryce in tow. They quickened their pace and exited through the west door. In the parking lot, they jumped in the van and exploded in celebration.

"We did it. Harding is gone!" Eri screamed to Charlie, hugging him once the van door was slammed closed.

Tears cascaded down Laura's cheeks. Bryce hugged her and kissed her. They whispered to each other.

Charlie reached to pull Eri into his lap, almost knocking over his laptop. "Are you ready to try normal."

She smiled. "Just tell me when."

Chapter Thirty-Five

Myers felt the exuberance the team felt, but once all of them coupled off to hug and kiss, a great weight of sorrow plummeted his chest. How he wanted to celebrate this with *her*. Denise's face shot through his memory, but then he saw Helena's face through the cloud. What was that about? He blinked to clear his memory back to Denise. But for some reason, he wanted to share it with Helena, too. Guilt tugged at his insides. How could he be thinking of someone else? So soon? It had only been a few months.

Laura dropped into the passenger seat and faced him. "How are you?"

His eyes burned. He blinked back the tears that threatened to fall and glanced her way, before looking back to the road. "It's hard."

She touched his arm. "This celebration is for her, too."

He nodded. Did he tell her? Laura had become a big sister or mom figure in his life. The trust and bond went deep. "I'm conflicted." He glanced her way.

She titled her head with furrowed brows. "How so?"

Could he say it? His tongue felt heavy in his mouth, his throat dry. "To move on."

Laura stared at him a moment before answering. "Helena."

He nodded, not looking. Not wanting to see the disappointment.

"Let me ask you a question. Do you think Denise would want you sad and alone, or happy with someone we all approve of?"

Thoughts of his crazy girlfriend filtered through his mind. If she was here, she would have no problem telling him what was what. Never did she hold back. If she could look down on him, she would probably be hitting him upside the head. "I'm not sure about the moving on, but I know she would want me to be happy."

"Does Helena make you happy?"

The question was simple, yet complicated. Her long, silky black hair, flawless olive complexion, gorgeous smile complete with dimples, and bright, playful brown eyes—there was attraction. But it was more than that. The harsh few months had allowed them to grieve together and connect in a strong way. Yes, there were feelings there. They weren't like what he had for Denise, but in their own way, they were stronger.

"Yes," he said simply.

"Then don't feel guilty, Myers. Life is too short." She kissed his cheek and moved to join her husband in the back.

Life was too short. Theirs likely shorter than others. Charlie had joked about finding normal. Normal was a city in Illinois, not an adjective to describe their lives. Too much had revealed itself to them. They had seen more than dreams could filter. Most likely, they would always be running. And maybe that was their normal.

"You know, Christmas is coming soon," Eri said from the back. "We need to find some place to celebrate."

"Preferably back in the country," Charlie said.

"Really, you want that?" Eri laughed. "What about your technology?"

"That's what satellites are for. So, not to worry."

Myers thought back to their last country trip. It had been nice. There he had become Helena's friend. "I agree. We need to disappear to some cabin somewhere." He pulled up to the warehouse and honked twice.

Antonio's guy opened the door, and they rolled in. Helena and Alicia stood just inside.

Myers turned off the engine, jumped out, and ran to her. He scooped her up, spun her around, and touched his lips to hers. She kissed back. It felt right. He pulled back and smiled. "We did it."

"You did!" She kissed him again and hugged him tight. "I knew you would. I'm so happy."

Myers pulled back as the group approached, but still held onto Helena's hand, and turned to Alicia. "How are you doing?"

"I'm good. I've been taking care of Teddy. He eats a lot."

Everyone laughed.

"Well," Laura said, "We have three things we need to do."

The team all looked to her.

"We need to celebrate!"

Everyone cheered.

"We need to help Antonio."

The group mumbled "yeah."

"And finally, we need to figure out where we want to live during the holidays. Well, we'll do it in that order." Laura waved at a spread Helena and Alicia had prepared for them. "Let's eat."

Myers took Helena's hand and led her to the table. It was covered with meats, cheeses, all types of breads and olives, and drinks. "This is beautiful." He looked at her. "As are you."

She smiled and placed a head on his shoulder. "I don't care where we go, as long as it is with you."

He tipped her chin up and lightly kissed her lips. "I feel the same."

Helena bit her lip. "And you're okay...I mean, with...her...I mean...?"

The question shocked his system a bit, but less than he would have thought. He wrapped her hands in his and held them to his chest. "I know she would want me to be happy. And you make me happy."

She kissed his cheek and smiled. "I agree."

"Hey, love birds." Charlie stood next to them with a plate. "You think you could move so some of us can eat?"

They laughed. "Let's eat."

As they moved together to get in line for food, his heart swelled. Though everything wasn't perfect, it was better.

Epilogue

Laura handed Antonio the thumb drive and nodded. "It's all there."

He stuck out his hand, and she shook it firmly. "You will always have a friend here."

"Ditto." She smiled.

"You know where you guys are going?" He glanced at the group that now included Willow, Deshawn, Teddy, and a girl named Kelsey. The four of them didn't have families to return to and decided to join the fight.

"We'll take it one day at a time." She slapped his back and walked to the van. "You all ready to roll? We have some deliveries to make." The plan was simple. Return everything they had stolen, either in person or money in the mail. It wouldn't be easy, but with S.I.U.'s bank now sitting in their own personal Cayman account, the world was theirs to take—or put back.

Charlie started the engine and backed out. The group sat around the van hip-to-hip, toe to toe. It was good to see everyone in good spirits. She especially liked her new friends. They fit in well. Teddy would be a handful, but his joy was contagious.

Bryce stretched and brought her into his embrace. She rested her head on his chest. "You ready for a real honeymoon? By old standards, we aren't officially married yet," he whispered.

She giggled. It was true. They hadn't had time to become a real married couple yet. "I think we can make that work at some point."

He kissed the top of her head and closed his eyes. For once, she didn't feel lost. Her family was right here. And they had a place—with each other—and no matter where they went, they would be okay. Of this, she was sure.

A word about the authors...

Kimberlee Mendoza is the recipient of the Sherwood Eliot Wirt Writer of the Year for 2007 for all of San Diego County. She is currently a Humanities professor at San Diego Christian College, a cover artist for The Wild Rose Press, Inc., and an author of over nineteen novels and fifteen plays. She is a graduate from Longridge Writing Group, has a BA in Human Development, a MA in Humanities, and is finishing her Ph.D. in Leadership.

~*~

Richard Mendoza III is Kimberlee's son. He is a graduate of San Diego School of Performing Arts and is currently studying for a BA in Communications at San Diego Christian College. He has won several district and national awards for his writing at the annual Fine Arts Festivals.

Thank you for purchasing
this publication of The Wild Rose Press, Inc.

If you enjoyed the story, we would appreciate your
letting others know by leaving a review.

For other wonderful stories,
please visit our on-line bookstore at
www.thewildrosepress.com.

For questions or more information
contact us at
info@thewildrosepress.com.

The Wild Rose Press, Inc.
www.thewildrosepress.com

Stay current with The Wild Rose Press, Inc.

Like us on Facebook

https://www.facebook.com/TheWildRosePress

And Follow us on Twitter
https://twitter.com/WildRosePress

Secrets of the Righteous

by

H. B. Berlow

The Ark City Confidential
Chronicles, Book 2

Secrets of the Righteous

COPYRIGHT © 2018 by Hugh Berlow and Shelia Hammer Family Revocable Trust

Contact Information: info@thewildrosepress.com

Cover Art by *Tina Lynn Stout*

The Wild Rose Press, Inc.
PO Box 708
Adams Basin, NY 14410-0708
Visit us at www.thewildrosepress.com

Publishing History
First Mainstream Historical Edition, 2018
Print ISBN 978-1-5092-2090-8
Digital ISBN 978-1-5092-2091-5

The Ark City Confidential Chronicles, Book 2
Published in the United States of America